"I'm eager to learn your ways," Orchid said.

"You'll learn. You are, as you say, a gifted student," replied John Eagle.

Then the lovely girl spoke quietly. "Speak to me of matters concerning love."

Eagle could hear Merlin's warning again: *You're to keep your hands off the girl.*

But what a girl she was, and very persuasive! Soon the Expeditor found himself saying, "I think we have a little time, you and I, to explore your education."

As she moved toward him, her fingers unzipping the front of her suit, Merlin's warning became fainter and fainter!

HAVE YOU READ ALL THE JOHN EAGLE—EXPEDITOR BOOKS?

#1 NEEDLES OF DEATH

#2 THE BRAIN SCAVENGERS

#3 THE LAUGHING DEATH

#4 THE FIST OF FATIMA

#5 VALLEY OF VULTURES

#6 THE GLYPHS OF GOLD

#7 THE ICE GODDESS

THE
DEATH
DEVILS

PAUL EDWARDS

 PYRAMID BOOKS • NEW YORK

THE DEATH DEVILS

A PYRAMID BOOK

Produced by Lyle Kenyon Engel

Copyright © 1974 by Lyle Kenyon Engel

Pyramid edition published October 1974

SBN 0-515-03366-9

Library of Congress Catalog Card Number: 74-11928

Printed in the United States of America

Pyramid Books are published by Pyramid Communications, Inc.
Its trademarks, consisting of the word "Pyramid" and the portrayal
of a pyramid, are registered in the United States Patent Office.

Pyramid Communications, Inc., 919 Third Avenue,
New York, N.Y. 10022

TABLE OF CONTENTS

CHAPTER 1 9
CHAPTER 2 13
CHAPTER 3 26
CHAPTER 4 37
CHAPTER 5 43
CHAPTER 6 54
CHAPTER 7 66
CHAPTER 8 76
CHAPTER 9 84
CHAPTER 10 95
CHAPTER 11 106
CHAPTER 12 117
CHAPTER 13 129
CHAPTER 14 142
CHAPTER 15 154
CHAPTER 16 161
CHAPTER 17 179

PROLOGUE

The woman he knew as his only mother was old, but as straight and dignified as a white birch. She was happy, White Deer was, that he had come once again to ask her to leave the Apache reservation which was her chosen home. She loved this tall dark-haired young man as if he had come from within her own womb instead of the womb of the white woman; the mother whose soft blue eyes were so much of the character in his own face. But now as she looked into his eyes, she saw things there—hard edges in his eyes and in his face.

"I have not asked you about your work, John. I have never asked, because I know that, true to the spirit of our people, the work you do could be nothing except honorable. But I have seen the faces of many warriors in my time, and I know the signs. You have killed, John."

"That is true, Mother." His eyes did not flinch from hers, a sign which helped to satisfy her heart.

"More than once you have killed. I think that you have killed many times."

"That is also true."

She looked at this black-haired young man whose skin was not white but somewhere between the sun-warmed hue of the white man and the darker skin of the Apache. She looked at him with love and with concern, because she knew what the constant bringing of death to others had done to the hearts and spirits of other warriors in by gone days.

"And the people you have killed—have they deserved death from your hands?"

He answered quietly. "Yes, my mother."

"And who decides whom you will kill? Yourself?"

"No. Another. Another for whom I work."

She was silent for a time, but her eyes remained upon his. "He is a good man, this man for whom you kill? He does not order the deaths of innocent people?"

"He does not order—and I do not execute—the deaths of innocent people."

She nodded. "But my first question, John. Is this man a good man?"

"A good man," he repeated. "That is a question I cannot truly answer."

CHAPTER 1

"I warned them. Damn it to holy hell, I warned them!"

The elderly man with the white hair and the bull-like shoulders moved from behind his ornate desk with short, impatient thrusts of his hands upon the rims of his wheelchair. As he approached the great glass window which faced the Hawaiian island of Maui, his frown deepened. It was the beginning of a nice day on Maui, the clear skies accepting with gratitude the coming of a benevolent dawn.

He snorted to himself. Here in this place—here at the uppermost portion of a fortress of more than forty rooms, laboratories, apartments and tunnels, designed and built by this frowning man within the yawning black maw of the dead crater of Makaluha—there were no beginnings of a nice day, not today anyway, and there was no feeling of benevolence. Right now, there was only anger.

"I told them," he said through his teeth. Then he turned to the woman.

"Yes, Merlin. You told them. You warned them."

Polly Perkins. Terrible name for a lovely woman.

The tight lines of Merlin's face loosened a bit—just a bit. She had that effect on him. This woman in her forties had possessed the ability to soften this hard man for many years. One eighth Hawaiian, the rest French and Anglo-Saxon, she was beautiful, loyal, and, as now, efficient.

"Merlin. The Secretary called again. He said it's urgent."

Merlin's frown deepened. "The same matter?"

"I believe so. He again referred to the conversation you and he had some six months ago. Regarding agriculture, he said."

Merlin nodded. "I want to hear the tape. You know which one."

"Yes, sir. I know precisely which one. But the Secretary is awaiting your call."

"I know that, Polly. Let him wait a bit longer. I've waited six months for his." She turned to the wall where she slid back a panel and touched three dials. In a matter of moments, she told him it was ready.

"Fine. I want it played. But first, if it's not too much trouble, could you pour me a bit of brandy."

"It's just a little early," she said. But she was already moving toward the door to her outer office when he responded:

"Not early, Polly. I'm hoping to hell that it isn't too late."

Alternating voices on stereo eight-track audio tape: the man known only as Merlin to all but a very few individuals—and one of those individuals, the Secretary of Defense of the United States of America:

Merlin: I don't like it, Mr. Secretary. I don't like it at all.

Secretary: Your problem is that you're an old war horse. You've got to realize that there are some areas

10

in which exchange of information can take place with no problems of security. It's a new era, Merlin.

Merlin (a sardonic laugh): Whose press notices have you been reading?

Secretary: All right. I'll admit we're not overly eager to show them the latest missiles we've developed but this is different. The Department of Agriculture—and some others—has had each of these men checked out thoroughly. Each is an eminent scientist whose only activity in the past twenty or more years has been involved with some aspect of making Chinese farms yield more crops. They are here to study our methods first hand—our *agricultural* methods. I frankly fail to see the possible security risk that's got you so fired up. Even if there were something to be seen which might compromise us—and there is *not*—they'll all be watched like hawks.

Merlin: Hawks. I was beginning to figure you for a *dove,* myself.

Secretary: Merlin—

Merlin: I still don't like the smell of it. I didn't call you on the phone based on nothing but a whim, Mr. Secretary—

Secretary: Then what would you call it?

Merlin: A hunch. An educated hunch, a mixture of experience and some nagging thought tugging at the back of my brain. I can't be more clear than that, but I simply don't like it!

Secretary (a sigh): I hope, Merlin, that it comes as no surprise to you that we can't—the United States can't—frame its entire foreign affairs program on nothing more than hunches. Your hunches and my hunches, both are included. A hunch is a hunch, but no more than that.

Merlin: And no *less* than that. But be that as it may, my friend, I've got another hunch which I don't mind sharing with you. I've got a real strong feeling

11

that within the year I'll be hearing from you—or maybe your boss—about this little tour our Chinese brothers are taking now. And when I do, you'll be agreeing with me. Only then, it just might be too late.

Secretary (levelly): If you get that call, Merlin—if it comes one night, real late so that you curse your way to the telephone—then I hope you take the proper amount of pleasure in it. I hope you gloat your way to hell and back!

Merlin laughed sharply. "At least he hoped I'd return."

Polly nodded. "I'll put the call through, Mr. Merlin."

He nodded, lifting the candle-warmed snifter of brandy to his lips. Gloating? He didn't feel like it, not at all. The fact that the Secretary was calling him now —and on this matter—did not bode well at all. As for going to hell and back, he himself couldn't make the trip. Somebody else would be doing so.

He nodded again, this time to himself. Yes. After he'd spoken with the Secretary, there would be a second telephone call.

Too bad, too. John Eagle was no doubt enjoying his much-needed vacation. But then, what else was an Expeditor for?

CHAPTER 2

Cyril Compton felt the goose bumps rise on his flesh and the attendant chill run down—or was it up?—his backbone. It was eight-thirty in the evening and, as he sat at the bar at Hong Kong's Mandarin Hotel, he felt extremely ill at ease. And why not? Why shouldn't he be nervous? After all . . .

He was forty-two years old. He didn't look his age, no. He told himself that now as he checked out his face in the mirror behind the bar. It was a strong face, even if the hair on top had thinned out a bit and the skin under the jawline had queerly bulged out to make it look as if it were a repository for excess weight. The large handlebar mustache had helped a bit, he thought, but maybe he'd been wrong about growing it. It might well be that if he shaved it off he'd look ten years younger. Once, when he was in college, in fact, he'd grown a beard and it had added several years to his appearance. He wondered. Maybe, if he shaved off the mustache . . .

He'd worry about that when he got home. New York. Tough place to keep in shape, New York, but he walked three miles daily—a mile and a half each way to and from work. Good exercise. The best. Walking. He'd read that in a magazine in his doctor's office. Or was it somewhere else?

He took a fast gulp of his martini, swallowing at least half of it. *What in blazes was he doing?*

Lord, here he was—in Hong Kong! Halfway around the world from New York. Halfway around the *universe* from his birthplace of Rawlins, Kansas. His very first trip outside of the United States, in fact, and here he was. In Hong Kong, B.C.C., *British Crown Colony*. He'd read that in the literature on the airplane. A 747. One of the biggest—and he, Cyril Compton, had flown on it. Part way, at least. And here he was—in Hong Kong, B.C.C. Would the folks back home or in the office be stunned . . .

He downed the rest of his martini and signaled for the yellow-skinned bartender. The bartender appeared not to notice him. Cyril Compton knew the man had seen him, but he was being snubbed, he knew that too. Always it was the same. Even at the office, but this time he had them—he really had them all! Sure, there were a lot of salesmen who had traveled all over the globe to sell the company's products, but this time *they* weren't interested in talking to a salesman. *They* wanted technical expertise. And, whether the salesmen—or in real fact the management—liked it or not, there was only one man with Wenona Chemicals Inc. who had the specific kind of technical expertise that *they* wanted.

Cyril Compton.

Himself.

Yet it was somewhat disturbing. Not the being chosen part; that was—well—recognition. The executives, hadn't really wanted to send him, but they had no choice. They would have liked to have gone themselves, but they knew it wasn't possible. Not if they wanted the sale. The sale. He wondered if he could

14

swing it. Possibly . . . no, that was the wrong attitude. The company's products were good. He ought to know, right? Right. If *they* wanted technical details, he could supply them—and also he would know exactly which details *not* to supply. *They* supposedly were very good at that—asking enough questions to get the answers so that they no longer needed a Cyril Compton or a Wenona Chemicals Inc. and could go ahead and do the whole thing themselves.

But suppose they *tortured* him for the information?

He lifted his glass again to his lips, but there was nothing in it.

"Waiter!" he said. When the slant-eyed man looked at him—somewhat crossly, Compton thought—he remembered. The man wasn't a waiter, just as he wasn't a salesman. "Er, *bartender*—er, yes. Bartender."

"Another?" the bartender asked.

Odd how these yellow-skinned people spoke perfect English. He would have expected—*had* expected—something different. Some kind of accent, a Chinese accent. Whatever that was.

"Another?" the bartender repeated. Compton looked at the man's white jacket, saw the name plate there. *Lee*.

"Hey," he said. "You know, back in the States, we had this civil war. And there was this general—"

The bartender smiled, but it was a bored smile. "His name was Robert E. Lee. He fought for the South. Yes, I know all about him. No, I'm no relation."

Cyril Compton tried to grin and failed. "Others have commented—"

"Once a week. At the very least, sir," the bartender said coolly. "Now—would you care for another martini?"

"Er, yes. But—"

The yellow man's eyebrows raised.

"But take it easy on the vermouth this time—got it?"

The bartender smirked, or at least Cyril Compton thought so. "Got it—*man*." He turned his back on the mustachioed American, who in turn smirked back, then looked at his image in the mirror.

The chill went down his spine again. This time it wasn't merely the result of being in a strange place—or even the elegant women in their sexy tight-fitting dresses with those slits up the sides which showed just enough to . . .

But you didn't dare try anything, you know? Cyril Compton knew. He knew that if he tried anything, one of them would have a boyfriend right at the next table and he'd take after Compton with a hatchet. Like in the old tong wars. Cyril Compton didn't know an awful lot about the tong wars but he knew they were Chinese. And he also knew that the Chinese all knew karate and judo and other devastating kinds of physical violence. Well, probably not all of them did, not everybody that was Chinese, but you could never tell.

But that had nothing to do with the latest spinechill nor the renewed gooseflesh he felt all over him.

The cause was the man sitting across the room. Compton could see him in the mirror, sitting there at a table slowly sipping his drink. It was the same man, Compton was sure of it.

He was a tall man, young and trim. Powerful looking, but not like a weightlifter. Black hair and blue eyes and skin that looked smooth but hard as steel. Tanned skin, almost the color of the suit he wore, a well-tailored suit without a visible crease other than those which were supposed to be there. The man smiled now as the waitress caught his attention. Very friendly the waitress was, but she would be to someone like that. She—and no doubt other women as well—

16

would find his face handsome. Handsome in a kind of animal way. No, none of the women here would call to a boyfriend if that man made any advances. And even if she did, he looked like he could take care of himself, even if the boyfriend did have a hatchet or a knife or something.

But that wasn't the point.

What *was* the point was that the man, just a split second ago, had been watching *him*. And it wasn't the first time. No, he'd seen the same man—looking at *him*—in the lobby when he'd crossed it to enter the bar. The man had been standing by the desk, reading a newspaper, or that's what he was supposed to be doing. But Compton had felt his eyes on him. He *knew* the man was watching him, he could *feel* it!

Just as a moment ago—

"Your martini, sir," the bartender said.

"Er, yes. Thank you." But Compton's eyes remained on the mirror. The man he watched was placing some money down on the table. He was standing. Yes, it was the same man, the very same—

He was coming this way!

Compton grabbed for the stem of his glass so quickly that in doing so half of the liquid spilled from it. That didn't matter, though, the thing being that he had to act natural. As he thrust the lip of the glass between his lips, he took a large swallow of the gin and vermouth. Damn it, too much vermouth again! But no matter, no matter—

He realized when he opened his eyes that they had been closed, that the muscles of his jaws were tightly clenched. How stupid of him, how really stupid! But as his eyes opened he discovered that the tall man was not standing behind him as he had expected. And as he looked around him, there was no trace of the man.

"Another?"

17

Compton looked at the bartender as if he were speaking another language, then he understood the question. "Er, no. I think maybe I've had enough. Thank you."

His tip might have been overly generous or insulting, he didn't know. He hadn't yet figured out the Hong Kong money. Roughly five Hong Kong dollars to one U.S. dollar, yes, he knew that—but how much a big or a little tip was over here he didn't know.

He stood, replacing his money in his billfold, then he started out of the bar.

What now, he wondered to himself. He only had this one night here in the British Crown Colony, and by rights he ought to wander around and see the sights. But Cyril Compton didn't want to do that. No, that wasn't true. He *did* want to. It was just that he was . . .

Admit it, you're afraid. Afraid to go out into the unknown.

Yes. Afraid. And tomorrow—

Tomorrow he was going north. By special invitation he, Cyril Compton, representing Wenona Chemicals Inc., was going north. Into Red China.

He shook his head. Mustn't call it that up there. They didn't like it, at least he didn't think they did. He'd listened to the briefing he'd received with his mind firmly planted in some old movie where the great philosopher Confucius was being machine-gunned by hordes of the Red Guard. Come to think of it, if they called themselves the *Red* Guard, what did they have against somebody referring to *Red* China? Or had all that been explained to him? Maybe. The problem was—

As he stepped across the lobby toward the desk, the problem, whatever it might have been, was replaced with another.

The man in the tan suit. He was by the door, seemingly looking at nothing, but Compton knew better.

18

He made his decision right then and there. He knew how he was going to spend the night.

In his room. In bed.

At somewhere between nine and nine-fifteen—he said later that he didn't know the exact time ("Why *should* I, for God's sake?")—the knock came on the door of his room.

"Y-yes?" He had taken off his coat and shirt and was reaching for his bag, which contained his bathrobe. "Who is it?"

The voice had an oriental lilt to it. "Bell captain, sir. You left something behind at the bar this evening."

His wallet! Of course. He'd been so preoccupied down there that he'd left it on the bar. Sure, he remembered taking out the money and putting it back.

He unlatched the lock on the door, then he remembered something else. He'd put the wallet back into his jacket pocket—the inside pocket where he always carried it. He was sure of it! And, yes, as he looked to where his coat lay on the bed, there it was, right where—

"Good evening, Mr. Compton."

The persistent voice riveted his attention back to the door. It was open now, but just for a moment.

The man in the tan suit closed it behind him.

"Wha—"

"Do not cry out, Mr. Compton," the man said, reaching into his jacket pocket. In the other hand, he held a slim attaché case. "My instructions are not to harm you—unless it is necessary. You will not make it necessary, will you?"

"I—"

But that's as far as Cyril Compton got. The man came at him like lightning, something flashing in his right hand. *A knife!* But no—it wasn't a knife. It was—

19

For the record, it was a syringe, a very small one. But its contents were effective enough to force Cyril Compton to unconsciousness an instant after the substance had entered his left shoulder.

John Eagle eased the other man back onto his bed, then looked about the room for the door key. It was on the long desk-bureau by the wall opposite the window. Picking it up, he dropped it into the pocket which held the syringe and left the room, careful to lock the door behind him.

He took the elevator down to the ground floor and stepped resolutely to the desk.

"I'll be checking out tomorrow," he said. There was no trace of the assumed accent to his voice now. "I'll be getting an early start and would like to pay my bill now."

The clerk looked up at him. "Ah, yes. You're Mr.—er—"

"Soames. Eric Soames." And, according to the forged American passport he carried with him, he was entirely correct.

"Yes, Mr. Soames." The man behind the desk totaled the bill for two nights and gave Eagle the receipt. "We hope you enjoyed your stay at the Mandarin, sir, and also hope that you'll visit our affiliated hotels at other stops in your travels."

Eagle paid the bill in Hong Kong cash and nodded. Inwardly, he smiled. Where he was going, there were no Mandarin-affiliated hotels. Although it was a certainty that he might enjoy such a luxury.

He took his change and went back to the bank of elevators. As the door to one of them opened, a beautiful Chinese girl with long legs strutted out, giving him an appreciative glance as she did.

The girl was another luxury he might well enjoy, but not right now. In between the times he was playing the roles Merlin laid down for him, maybe. But not

20

now. Now he was *earning* all that money the old man was paying him.

He smiled again, this time outwardly. No, he wasn't really earning his keep this night. Tomorrow, however . . .

Out of the elevator and to Compton's door. He inserted the key and turned it until the telltale *click* told him that the door was unlocked. Then he opened the door and closed it behind him.

Compton still lay where he had been placed. Face down. Fine, except that for the present business it wasn't fine.

Eagle easily lifted the man from the bed and sat him in a chair to the side of the desk-bureau. He placed another chair in front of the mirror over the desk and sat in it. Looking into the glass, he observed the angle of Compton's face. He stood and made a slight adjustment. Fine.

Then he brought the attaché case to the desk and opened it.

There were a number of glass jars, filled with light-colored substances. He sat down, opening two of the jars. He looked at Compton, then at his mirror image.

"Goodbye, Eagle—hello, Compton," he said softly. "Goodbye, Expeditor. Hello, chemical salesman."

In half an hour it was done. The unique plastic substances and makeup that he used were developed in Merlin's Makaluha laboratories. Although Merlin had profited from his knowledge of Hollywood makeup expertise, the fast drying and permanent nature of the stuff the Expeditor had splashed and molded on his face was unknown to the film trade. And for a very good reason. Capturing a likeness on film—even the truest color film available—demanded a certain amount of naturalness. But the human eye is ten times as sen-

21

sitive when it comes to what people in the business call makeup. And now, right now, the human eye—an eye other than Eagle's or Compton's—couldn't tell the two of them apart.

John Eagle, Expeditor, had become Cyril Compton, chemicals expert. Facially the remake was thorough. Now to see about the rest.

Eagle stripped to his undershorts and dressed in the unconscious man's clothes. The trousers were far too large, but there was enough plastic in the tubes to make up for part of the difference. As for the rest, the hell with it, the coat would hide it. The shirt fit all right, although the neck size was a bit loose while the jacket was a bit snug around the shoulders, but it would do. He smiled to himself as he placed a pair of Compton's argyle socks on his feet, then he considered the man's shoes. They were wrong, all wrong. He'd take the chance with his own black three-quarter boots. They were British made and could have been purchased in any one of several countries—therefore, no problem when he'd have to leave them behind.

He looked at his watch, then at the unconscious Compton. It was almost ten. Eagle checked out his reflection in the full-length mirror which was part of the bathroom door. Then he left the room, locking the door behind him.

"I'm Cyril Compton," he told the clerk behind the desk in the lobby. It was the same man he'd spoken to earlier as Eric Soames.

"Yes, Mr. Compton. How can I help you?"

"My room. I'll be needing it for another day. I hope there won't be any problem."

The clerk considered and checked his wallboard. "You're fortunate, sir. We had a last-minute cancellation. This time of year, you know—the Fair. Well, every hotel room in Hong Kong is occupied—"

"Except for the one cancellation," Eagle said.

22

"Yes, except for that. A single room. Yes." He looked at the mustachioed man with curiosity. "A change in plans, sir?"

"A slight one, yes."

As Eagle re-entered the elevator, he smiled to himself. The last-minute cancellation the deskman was referring to was probably that of Eric Soames. Even if in the interim Soames' room had been slated for another occupant, arrangements had been made for two additional last-minute cancellations. Two of Merlin's agents—one in Singapore, the other in Sydney—had just wired the hotel with regrets that their plans had changed.

Cyril Compton was awake when Eagle locked the door behind him.

The man's eyes stared unbelievingly, moving with him as he moved to the chair before the mirror and sat down facing the chemicals expert. Except for his eyes, Compton was motionless. It was the way the serum Eagle had injected into the man was supposed to work. Complete paralysis of all motor faculties, except for the eyes and other sensory organs. The man could see and hear; otherwise he seemed constructed of stone.

Eagle smiled at the man whose face he wore. *"Nyet Nyeh probeevityeh dveegawtsyah."* Then he frowned. "Excuse me. I know you do not speak my language," he said in the foreign accent he'd used previously. "I said that you should not try to move. You cannot. Tell me, are you frightened? Just blink your eyes twice for yes, once for no."

Compton's eyes blinked rapidly. Twice.

Eagle nodded. "That is very good, Mr. Compton. If you are frightened you perhaps will not do anything which will force me to kill you. I have been given no orders to kill you, and therefore it would not be professional of me to do so. Personally, I would just as soon see you dead, but then such things are not up to me to decide. As you have your superiors in your place of business, I also have mine. On behalf of my superiors, I must beg your pardon for perhaps undermining a possible sale of your company's products on the other side, but such a sale is not of much consequence compared to the job which I—you—will accomplish once there. Would you like to know what that job is?"

Compton's eyes again blinked. Once.

Eagle laughed. "A correct response. As you say in your own country, what you do not know cannot harm you. In any event, sometime tomorrow morning you will awaken to find yourself in the clothes closet. You will be tempted to rush to the authorities with the story of what has happened to you. I trust you will think twice before doing so. We have people everywhere. The local police are not to be trusted. As for the American consulate, I would not suggest your going there. They will already be searching for you, you see. Because their reports will show that you—or rather a man with your face—will have done something a bit embarrassing to the spirit of cooperation which prevails between your country and the one which lies north of here. I trust you understand me?"

One eye-blink.

"No?"

Two eye-blinks.

"Good. Very well, then. You and I have nothing more to discuss and, since what I crave now is some vodka from room service, I think it is time we say our goodbyes."

As Eagle rose from his chair, Compton's eyes grew wide. They closed two seconds after the small syringe was plunged into his arm.

Making the unconscious man as comfortable as he could in the closet, Eagle next moved to the man's attaché case and removed the important papers. He

24

already carried Compton's passport in the suit jacket, but there were other papers—

Yes. The three-ring binder filled with product specifications. That was transferred to Eagle's own slimmer case. And the most important piece of paper of them all.

The official invitation from the People's Republic of China to one Cyril Compton of Wenona Chemicals Inc. to attend the Canton Trade Fair. The Expeditor's tickets into the beginning of Red country. *Operation Orchid,* Preparatory Phase One, was complete. But there was something he wanted to do before getting the sleep his mind told him his body would be thankful for the following day.

He had to practice. He'd practiced the whole routine for a couple of hours back at Camp Three, but this was the first time he'd be doing it with the clothes he'd actually be wearing. He'd even brought a stopwatch along for the purpose, and now, standing with his face to a blank wall, he clicked the button.

Then he undressed.

Shoes and socks went off together, then tie and shirt and jacket were pulled off in one fluid motion. The belt was loosened and fly zipped down simultaneously. Except for his shorts, Eagle was stark naked. Twenty-three seconds. Not bad, but not all that good either. Considering the motions which would follow his undressing, he'd have to cut it down. By a lot.

He dressed again.

And undressed again. Twenty-three seconds.

Eagle cursed.

And dressed again.

Merlin had laughed about the whole exercise. "Think of it as preparing for a quickie in your favorite massage parlor," he'd said.

"My tastes are a little more refined, I'm afraid," Eagle had replied.

"Excellent. I wouldn't want you sidetracked in the middle of this mission. Which reminds me. You're to keep your hands off the girl. Red Chinese morality being what it is, she's liable to be virgin *in tacto*. I want her kept that way, you understand? I know what you've done on other assignments, but not on this one. And not with this girl. I mean it, John."

"Constraint accepted," Eagle had said. "Your Orchid shall remain pure snowy white—if her morality wills it so."

Orchid. Orchid of Delight. Eagle thought about the name.

A promising name for a woman. As he got ready to thumb the stopwatch, he wondered whether the lady had the potential to live up to it.

CHAPTER 3

On the outskirts of the Kwangtung Province town of Shih-hsing, some one hundred and eighty miles from the place where John Eagle was thinking of her name, the young woman who owned that name stepped from her room in a dormitory which resembled a Quonset hut into the night outside the door. Even with the white laboratory coat which now clothed her, the Expeditor, could he have seen her now, would have agreed that on the basis of first appearances her name was a fitting one.

There is no lab coat in the world that has flattering properties, but in the careless way the girl had tightened the belt of the coat around her waist, her slender yet ample body had achieved without intention a sexuality which other women would have spent hours—paying some professional beauty expert's high rates—to even approach. It was almost a boyish figure, only an inch over five feet, and topped by a slender, swanlike neck which supported a delicate oval face. Her hair was short, tending to reinforce the boyish look, but one look into the large black eyes with their long graceful lashes disspelled any error one might be inclined to make about her sex. They were capable of worlds of emotion, those eyes, and now outside the dormitory the emotion they held was one of melancholy.

But not for long.

She had gone outside that night because it was warmer than usual. She had been working late and was tired, but somehow she didn't feel ready for sleep. Out there, that night, the stars were so very bright, clear as cool diamonds. It was almost as if the old stories were true, the old peasant stories about the stars really being the intelligent spirits of our ancestors, shining down for us to show us the proper way to conduct ourselves.

Superstition, of course. Foolish, unproductive superstition. Yet—it sometimes was nice to fantasize. Even if one's entire training was in the realm of scientific experimentation and theory and fact. Such was her training, yet such had been her father's training and he . . .

He had not dismissed the old stories so easily. "Think of them as you would think of other theories. Hypotheses, if you will, little Orchid. Unprovable, of

27

course, but all the same one cannot prove they are *not* right as well."

Her father. She now looked up at the twinkling stars.

"Are *you* up there, my father? Are you guiding my conduct? From somewhere on the other side of life, are you showing me the proper way to conduct myself?"

Such were her thoughts when she heard the movement of feet. The sound brought her back to reality. ("Define *reality*," her father had once insisted. "Reality is what is real," she had replied.)

The uniformed man who stopped before her now was real. So was his voice:

"Good evening, daughter of Yang," he said. Colonel Chou Ko-chu of the People's Intelligence Service—or whatever the correct title was, not that she cared— bowed slightly, taking her hand in his. His hand felt brittle. In fact, although Colonel Chou was a man in his early forties, *brittle* was an excellent word to describe him. Scarecrow thin, even his voice sounded as if it were composed of clinks and cracks which appeared as soon as the tone issued from between his lips.

The girl shivered as he pressed her hand between the two of his. "Colonel Chou," she said unemotionally. Her eyes, still round and large, looked now as if some transparent film covered them.

"My respects," the colonel said, releasing the hand. "And expressions of my sorrow."

"I have had time to adjust," she returned flatly.

"I realize that it has been three weeks since your esteemed father departed this life. I also realize that I should have come to you before this. But these are busy times and, as you know, I have been away from our installation. I sincerely regret the passing of the esteemed Dr. Yang, who—"

"You have been busy," she said.

She closed her eyes, as if savoring her grief.

After a while Colonel Chou said, "Our country will miss him. He was one of a kind. To your father, the people owe a great debt."

She smiled wistfully. "My father was happy working, happy serving his land and his people. He would feel that he is owed nothing."

"And you, little Orchid, you too are a creditor to the people's gratitude. Is there something that you wish?"

"Nothing, Colonel Chou. I, too, have my work."

He nodded. "But the project will not last forever. What will happen after its completion?"

"There will be other projects."

"I suppose there might be. But you could have more. If you chose to, that is."

She looked at him blankly. "I serve where I am needed, Colonel."

His eyes narrowed slightly. "That is not what I meant."

"I know."

He sighed. "Without a father, you need someone to look after you."

"I am twenty. I was raised to look after myself, Colonel."

"I meant, little Orchid, a man. Someone who, like your father, would look after—"

"There is no one like my father, Colonel Chou. As you yourself have said, he was one of a kind."

The eyes narrowed slightly more. "A woman such as yourself—she needs ... affection. A man to—"

"Colonel Chou, I suppose that you are correct. As a student of life forms, I am aware of the sexual needs of human as well as other creatures which walk our planet—and those which not only crawl upon its surface but burrow beneath it. I also, however, am aware of my own needs in that regard. At this time, I feel little need for male attention. My father has been absent

29

from me for less than a cycle of the moon. I have no need for any substitute."

"I was not speaking to you as one who would wish to father you."

"I am aware of that. But I am not ready yet for any kind of close male companionship."

He studied her for a moment. "But you do not close the door. I have admired you for some time, little Orchid. I would be pleased to have a closer relationship with you. I have much to offer, I assure you of that."

"No one would dispute the regard in which the people hold Colonel Chou," she said.

"Yet I feel that perhaps your father may not have liked me, perhaps not understanding the necessity for a position such as that filled by myself—"

"My father understood the necessities of life, Colonel. He recognized the people's need for your area of work."

"And he never spoke against me to you? Never—"

"Never." Her eyes flashed upward, as if asking the stars to forgive her for what was, in fact, a lie.

He smiled, again taking up her hand. "Then the door is not closed."

The smile she returned him was forced, but it was a smile. "There is no door which can be closed, Colonel, which cannot be opened by he who knows the proper way."

He released her hand. "Little Orchid, it warms me to hear words which I can take only as encouragement. It is, I think, very wise on your part to give me this encouragement. Tonight it is late, and I must see to my duties. But there will be other nights—nights when my duties will take care of themselves. Then, perhaps, we shall speak again. Then, I trust, my patience will bear fruit."

He bowed, a smile on his face. "It may have occurred to you that I am not an overly patient man. And in truth I am not. It is a personal failing that I—and others—have had cause to regret."

His exit line delivered with what he no doubt considered to be the proper weight he turned and walked briskly from the girl's presence.

Define reality, her father had insisted.

She lay now upon the single bed in her dormitory room. The room was small but sufficient to her needs. At least sufficient to her physical needs. As to the psychological, even the roof of the entire universe had not been enough earlier. There were physical realities and psychological realities and they need not be the same.

Reality is what is real, she had told her father. And he had laughed. It was both serious and good-natured, at one and the same time. Much of her father's actions and words combined the two attributes. He was seriously good-natured and good-naturedly serious, an excellent combination. She had, however, defended her reply:

"A devious question deserves an indirect answer," she had said, but he had disagreed.

"Directness, my daughter, is on the contrary the only proper response to the devious. In any event, your answer was far from indirect. It was as direct as they come. It is both true and meaningless. Sometimes, daughter, I tend to think the true and the meaningless are the same."

As the girl stared at the ceiling in her darkened room, she remembered vividly the night she and her father had had this discussion which, she suspected then—and many times since—had more meaning than a simple chat regarding philosophy. It had been less than two months ago, four weeks before. That was

31

when they had spoken of reality, but his mood had begun to change before that.

She had noticed it first when he returned from America. Of course he was flattered to be selected to make the trip and to be appointed the senior scientist of the group. Even thought he was the head of the project here, that did not necessarily mean that someone else—someone whose politics were a bit purer than Dr. Yang's—might not have been made senior man of the visiting group. And he had looked forward to making the trip, to see firsthand the America he'd heard so many conflicting things about. "The United States," he told his daughter before embarking, "must be the most evil place in the world and the best—if all we supposedly know of that country is true."

In one respect, at least, the Americans had done something very well. In the field of Dr. Yang and his daughter, they evidently had performed miracles. It was these miracles that the group of biologists and botanists, each a specialist in his field, were going to America to witness firsthand.

Their project involved the development of a special species of insect which would feed upon other insects which were harmful to agriculture and which, in fact, had been responsible for a good many crop failures. The project had, among its staff, all the skills requisite to do the job, but the Americans, it seemed, had been doing a great deal of work in insect genetic control and so, in the new spirit of cooperation between the East and West, a trip for observation purposes was arranged.

The enthusiastic Dr. Yang who departed his homeland, however, was not the same man who returned. He had changed, deep inside somehow, very subtly. It was as if he viewed his work differently now.

"But Father, it is extremely worthwhile, this work we do!" she had insisted. "What greater service to our people could we of science be, than to increase the yields of our land?"

"That would be a goal worthy of the greatest of efforts, my daughter, I quite agree. Yet, regarding this work we do, it seems to me there is somewhat more than readily meets the eye."

She looked at him oddly. "But you are the project head! Surely you are familiar with all of the work we are doing!"

"Surely," he had repeated slowly. "Yet there are many people here in our compound, many jobs being done. I get periodic reports on the progress being made, but . . ."

His voice had trailed off. "Tell me, my daughter, what there is about our project which would interest the likes of a Colonel Chou? Why is it that an officer of his rank would be assigned to command the nontechnical aspects of our work here?"

"It is not unusual for an army officer to—"

"But an officer in *intelligence*? No, there is something more to what we do. . . ."

She offered an explanation. "You went to America, Father. A group of our people went with you. Perhaps they are afraid that you or one of them might spread lies about the people there and other things you found about the place."

"Nonsense," he told her. "We are becoming friendly with the Americans. And I, for one, feel that it is about time. They are a good people, and my saying that does not contradict any of our current political truths. No, that is not the reason. I keep thinking of the basic purpose of our work. When all is said and done, it is *genetic control*. If, for example, what we are attempting to do—and probably will do—in our project with insects, if the same thing could be done effectively and selectively with *human beings . . .*"

33

His tone had frightened her. "You really think that—"

"I don't know. What I do know is that I had been thinking about Colonel Chou long before I traveled to the United States. What that man of twisted bamboo was doing here; I had thought long upon it. I have decided to know more."

"Father, you must be careful. If you should offend one of the ilk of Colonel Chou—"

He had laughed at her, but it was a serious laugh all the same. "I am an old man, my daughter, too old to offend anyone, I'm afraid. Besides, I shall do no more than I am supposed to do—look closely at the work which is my responsibility. I shall, however, be taking looks which are of closer scrutiny than those of the past." And then his face suddenly darkened.

"But, because I am old, daughter, I have made something of a precaution concerning you. Perhaps, when I am gone, little Orchid, you will think of leaving this place."

"This place? You mean Shih-hsing?" Somehow she did not think he was speaking of just the village. She was correct.

"No, daughter. I speak of China. I think you would like the United States and its people. I have a request to make of you."

She bowed in the outmoded old way. "Your request is my requirement, Father."

The bow was acknowledged by a soft hand upon hers. "You will begin to learn the English language. I have procured some books on the subject, supposedly to enable me to better understand the American entomological studies, but my purpose was you. You will master the language as quickly as possible. If something . . . should happen to me—"

"Father—"

"I say *if*. But if something *should* happen to me in

34

the near future, something . . . sudden . . . it may be that someone might come for you."

Someone might come.

Someone. If . . .

It had happened suddenly. Very suddenly, almost as if . . .

In several of the breeding cubicles there were tanks of hydrogen and oxygen to assist in the creation of stabilized atmospheres for the experimental larvae the scientists were hatching under specialized conditions. Dr. Yang had been inside one of these cubicles—alone—when for some reason one of the tanks exploded. The entire wing of the building was destroyed, just as if some kind of bomb—

But no—*no!* Over and over she'd told herself that. No. He had been too important a man and, even if he had not been of importance in the past, his current work . . .

But he had not known what that was, had he? Perhaps he had found out. And perhaps that was why—

No!

But she intensified her study of English, a difficult language for her to master. She had begun her study the very day her father had made his request, but after his death—his *sudden* death—

Someone might come. . . .

And now she rose from her bed. Trying to sleep was useless, but she did not want to go outside again. She knew he was out there somewhere, Colonel Chou Kochu. Instead, she contented herself to look out of her narrow window. She could see several of the metal buildings, those housing the scientists and technicians and those housing the insect life which was the reason for the project. Unless her father was right, unless there was another reason for the project.

She shook off the feeling, or tried to, concentrating

35

on the high wire fence surrounding the compound. The fence was electrified, and the four towers at points within the fence had as their main feature manned machine guns. Why? And why so many security guards? Colonel Chou's men.

Why?

Her father had perhaps been right to question the why of it all. Why should such a project as this demand such tight security measures? Why would such an effort be made to keep out prying eyes, to keep out any unauthorized . . .

Someone might come.

To take her away. That had been her father's meaning, she was sure of it. To take her away from her work, from her native land. Her old father might well have found America and its people to his liking, but *these* were her people, *this* was her land. Could she leave it—even if someone really *could*—

Someone.

She closed her eyes tightly, trying to imagine just what such a someone might look like.

CHAPTER 4

The man who carried the face and papers of Cyril Compton had his eyes closed as if he had been lulled to sleep by the click-clacking rhythm of the train as it rolled smoothly along rails of steel which, second by second, were taking him closer to his destination. Before the eyes had closed they checked the watch on his wrist, an inexpensive mass-produced American model that he was sure was, turning his wrist green. But no matter. The thing kept reasonably good time.

Two-fifteen in the afternoon. Almost time for Phase Three of *Operation Orchid* to be set into motion, and thus time to close the eyes, to gather into that part of the body—the lower stomach—the quiet strength which would give him the stamina to carry the thing through. Coming up was the beginning of the tough part. What had passed had been relatively easy.

After his business with the true Compton, he had slept, awakening early enough to leave the hotel casually, carrying nothing but his lean attaché case. Taking the Star Ferry from Hong Kong Island across Victoria Harbor to Kowloon, he'd gotten aboard a train surprisingly packed with Chinese and their belongings stuffed into baskets on the ends of dangerously wielded shoulder poles. For an hour and a half the uncomfortable train traveled north until it reached Lo Wu. Here everyone on the train disembarked, for although the steel tracks continued northward across the bridge which spanned the Sham Chun River, passengers could not make the crossing that easily.

Across the Sham Chun, across that bridge, was Communist territory.

The formalities on the British side were few. Passport checking, an explanation of his purpose for visiting the People's Republic. There was no luggage check. On the other side of the bridge, however, which all of those bound north reached by walking, things were a bit more thorough.

"The People's Republic welcomes you, Mr. Compton," said the customs official who examined passport and Fair invitation carefully, then peered into the open attaché case.

"Samples," Eagle said when the inspector peered at the small clear white-capped vials of green and purple liquid. "I'm representing a chemicals firm."

The officer nodded, then, after examining the pills and implements in Eagle's toilet kit, leafed through the ring-binder of specification sheets, pausing to look at one of the pages which, unlike the others, held a large paper clip at the top. There on the page were color drawings matching exactly the vials the man had inspected earlier. This particular page was the only one Eagle had inserted into Compton's book. If the inspector had not located it—although the clip had been placed there to draw his attention—Eagle would have located it for him.

The inspector's hands carefully checked out the sides of the case, looking for any hidden compartments. The compartments were there, very thin ones, but Eagle had been assured by its designer—one of Merlin's

38

specialists—that it had been thoroughly tested, one of the tests being a tip-off to the Honolulu customs officials that a fortune in gems was being smuggled into the U.S. by a man carrying just that bag. The resulting inspection had been most thorough, but the compartment (which in this instance contained nothing but folded cloth) remained undiscovered.

As it did now.

"Please enjoy your visit, Mr. Compton," the official said, turning to the next man in line. Within the hour, the cleaner and roomier train from the bridge to Canton pulled out to the tune of piped-in music which Eagle assumed was supposed to be both revolutionary and stirring.

End of Phase Two.

Eagle's eyes opened. Two-forty. It was time.

"Excuse me," he said to the business-suited man sitting next to him. A German, coming to Canton to discuss the intricacies of high-quality steel production, he'd told Eagle, who had pretended a mild sort of interest. Now, however, his apologetic look to the rear of the coach made it obvious that his own interests were more immediate. The restroom, of course.

As he stepped up the aisle, he noted that he was being watched by the green-uniformed soldier who stood directly before the restroom door. Through the glass door separating this car from the one behind it, Eagle could see two additional soldiers outside, one on the platform of each car. Three. That was the initial number to worry about. Except that there was no sense in worrying, not in this business.

He nodded politely to the soldier—an officer, by the absence of rifle and the fact he possessed a sidearm— and opened the door to the lavatory. Closing and snap-locking the door to the cramped quarters, he jammed himself into the door side right-hand corner of the room and waited.

That's all. He simply waited.

A minute passed. Then two.

Then came the polite tap of knuckles on the outside door. Eagle didn't stir, not a muscle of his body moved.

Thirty seconds passed, then the rap of the knuckles came a bit harder. Again Eagle did nothing, except to keep his eye on the sweep-second hand of the cheap watch on his wrist.

Ten seconds, and he heard the tiny *click* of something turning the snap-lock from the outside. Quietly the door opened outward.

The officer came in pistol-first, cautiously. Then, as Eagle's hand grasped his wrist, his movements were swift—too swift from his point of view.

"Vkhawdeetiyeh!" Eagle said. It was Russian for "Come right on in." The officer unwittingly obliged, his head colliding with the far wall of the lavatory a split second after Eagle had snapped his wrist. There was no time for a cry of pain, not even of surprise. The Chinese had slumped unconscious to the floor by the time Eagle had the door closed again. Working swiftly, he picked up his attaché case in his left hand and the officer's pistol in his right. It was a Russian Tokarev Model 30 or a Chinese imitation of the pistol which itself was a close imitation of the Browning automatic. It wasn't the best of weapons, but it would do. A matter of necessity.

He was about to open the door to the outside when he remembered. There was one more small detail to attend to. Placing the nose of the Tokarev under his armpit temporarily, he reached into his jacket pocket and pulled out a small white card. He checked the lettering to be certain.

CYRIL G. COMPTON
Wenona Chemicals Inc.

The New York address and telephone number appeared in the lower portion of the card, but he didn't think the Chinese would be interested in writing or phoning long distance. He crumpled the card slightly, then dropped it to the side of the commode.

Then he opened the door and stepped out of the lavatory.

Quickly his eyes determined that no one had yet missed the guard nor shown any interest in his quiet disappearance. But his eyes also determined something else. That portly man—an Englishman by the look of him—getting up from his seat toward the front of the car. He was turning this way. There would be only one reason for his doing so.

Eagle would have to work very fast now.

The automatic concealed under his briefcase, he opened the door to the outside platform. His manner was seemingly casual, merely a man wishing to stretch his legs. But inside his mind, he did not feel casual at all. He had made one slight miscalculation.

There were three guards outside.

He'd seen two of them before, one on each of the two connecting platforms. The third, on the other side, unlike the two he'd noticed, carried a sidearm rather than a rifle. The officer in charge of the other car, probably just stepping outside for a breath of fresh air. Or maybe a part of normal routine—to check that all was correct in the car ahead.

"Good morning," Eagle said to the nearest soldier, who was already shaking his head and beginning to gesture with the rifle which was intended to communicate the fact that passengers were not allowed out here. He did not, however, have time to complete the move before Eagle's bootsole had snapped up and collided full force against the man's chest. He had time for just a short scream before his weapon clattered to the platform and he himself went over the side railing to land

41

abruptly on some piece of landscape adjacent to the railway tracks.

Even before their soldier-comrade's hasty departure, the two Chinese on the opposite platform had come to realize that all was not as it should be. The rifleman took the Tokarev's first shot just to the side of his right eye, the second shot from Eagle's automatic driving its way through the officer's left temple. Neither man had a chance to get his weapon in a line where it would do any good. The officer's body slumped far to the right of the platform, out of the range of vision of anyone within either car. The rifleman's body unfortunately fell straight downward, in plain and easy sight of anyone looking—

But the hell with it. There wasn't anything Eagle could do about it now. He could throw both bodies from the platform, but that would take time. And time was something he knew he didn't have much of. Timing was critical now.

The ladder up the outside wall of the car made the climb to the top easy. Swiftly Eagle checked both directions as his eyes reached the top level of the car. No guard up there, none. He had been told in his briefing that in the old days all parts of the train were closely guarded. "But things have gotten a bit sloppy," the Chinese expert said. "After all, there's been little in the way of trouble on the train run for a long, long time."

Time.

Crouching on the car roof, Eagle stripped his belt from half of its loops. Running the leather through the handle of the attaché case, he pulled it tightly. The case was snug against his lower back as he refastened the belt on his stomach.

His eyes scanned the landscape ahead. Excellent. The terrain was very hilly. If he had taken too much time, he would have found himself surrounded by flat

42

land. He braced himself, waiting for the train to slow, He knew it would. In a matter of seconds, he was sure, either that Britisher would be shouting about the officer who had been left in the can—or else somebody would spot the dead soldiers below him on the platform.

His odds were on the Britisher, not that it mattered either way. Unless of course, the discoverers of the trouble announced their discovery with blasting rifles. His thoughts momentarily rested upon his naked skin. Not naked in the sense that he was not clothed, but in the sense that he was used to wearing a thin plastic suit which had the protective ability to withstand most any gunshot. That was the problem with entering a target area through "normal" means—customs inspections and all that.

Orchid of Delight.

She'd goddamned well better be worth it!

CHAPTER 5

"She's worth it," Merlin had said when Eagle had raised the point. "Besides, what have you got better to do?"

Sitting in the special Camp Three briefing room which lay under a span of sunburnt desert in Death

43

Valley, the Expeditor frowned at the wall before him. It was composed of several screens, some hooked into film and videotape banks here and others which direct-lined into other banks, one of which was located in the Makaluha fortress. Among the screens were ones which were glass-enclosed, while others were constructed of simple white canvas. Both front and rear projection units could operate simultaneously. It was a mixed media set-up which would make the entertainment world drool with envy, but entertainment was not the object. As the audio unit presented Merlin's question—no video; Eagle had never seen his employer's face and doubted he ever would—the Expeditor reflected that all of this was far from entertaining.

What did he have better to do? Merlin knew damned well the answer to that question. So did Samson, the man who earned his probably substantial salary by knowing where John Eagle was during his every moment of leisure. Four hours previous—in Manhattan—Eagle had heard the unwelcome sound of Samson's gritty but sympathetic voice over the telephone.

"Vigil Red," Samson said. "I hope I'm not interrupting anything."

Eagle looked from the bedside telephone to the bed and the lusciously nude girl who smiled at him invitingly. Eagle, too, was naked. He scowled.

"I don't believe it," he said.

"Don't believe what—that the call has come?"

"No. I believe that, all right. I just don't believe that you hope you're not interrupting. I think you enjoy it, Samson, I really do."

"I am deeply wounded," Samson replied. There was only a slight hint of sarcasm in his voice.

"Give me an hour," Eagle said.

"You know better than that." A pause. "Thirty minutes."

"You're all heart."

"You want to try for fifteen?"

"Thirty minutes," Eagle said. He hung up.

The girl repeated the two words, then sighed. "John, it's nine-fifteen in the morning. I took off work today, just so the two of us could—"

Eagle nodded, then he smiled at her. "Do I look unappreciative?"

She—her name was Natalie and she was a successful fashion designer—did not smile back. "The last time you were here, the same thing. This Mr. Samson, why don't you fire him?"

Eagle laughed. Little Natalie had no idea of the kind of business he was in, although she knew he must be successful at it. But she was right. It was a while back, the last time he had seen her, and although it was two in the morning when the call from Samson came, she remembered the name. When Eagle had called her, late last night, she had been delighted. He had done his best to delight her all night long. But this morning— that was to be her time for delighting him. Not that she hadn't done her share during the past hours. But he was looking forward to it.

And so was she.

"I've got thirty minutes," he said.

"I gathered that."

"Then do some additional gathering, while there's time."

She reached out to him and pulled him toward her.

Then she gathered him.

Expertly.

In the Camp Three briefing room, Eagle let his frown answer Merlin's question. The fact that his boss's visage was not being broadcast to him had nothing to do with his own not being telecast to Makaluha.

45

Eagle had, in fact, heard the familiar low hum from the wall which told him he was on camera.

What did he have better to do—indeed!

Merlin evidently found his reaction amusing. The old bastard laughed. "Come now, John. Skills are like muscles. Inactivity makes them go soft, lose their suppleness. How long has it been since your services have been required?"

"A little less than a month, sir," Eagle answered dryly.

"Obviously, it's time to flex again, John. I like that word. *Flex*. Conjures up quite a variety of connotations, doesn't it?"

"I suppose," Eagle said. *Flex you,* was what he thought. "I'm not that much of a grammarian."

"Which reminds me. You'll have to learn a couple of Russian phrases. I think it would serve our purposes to have our Chinese friends think it was our Russian friends who were responsible for the little thing which is your assignment. A language man will give you all you need before departure—which, by the way, is within six hours. Also an equipment man. Unfortunately, your mode of attack will be a little different this time. But enough about that."

And now Merlin got directly to the point. A face flashed onto a rear-projection screen. A Chinese, an elderly-looking man.

"Dr. Yang Kuan-hua," Merlin said. "An eminent entomologist, a brilliant man."

"Red Chinese," Eagle said.

"Yes, and dead."

The face of Dr. Yang disappeared. In its place on the screen was a photograph of a group of Chinese, some ten or eleven or twelve of them. Eagle saw that centrally placed in the group was the man whose face he'd just seen.

"Some six months ago, John, this group came to the

46

United States to study certain methods our country has been using to protect crops from the ravages of insect life. I won't go into all the details, but I think the important fact is that the one method which the group was most interested in was our use of insects—insects which were carefully developed to destroy other insects which kill valuable plant life. If you wish, I have full details on a tape which I can play for you."

"Not yet," Eagle said.

"Good. At the time this group made its visit, I protested to the Defense Secretary. To no avail, as it turned out. There was no possible problem in connection with national security, he told me. I didn't see it that way, and it turns out I was right."

Eagle thought of expressing his congratulations, and also thought Merlin had paused for the very purpose of allowing him to do so. He said nothing, merely waited.

A new photograph went on the screen. An enlarged insect. "This," Merlin's voice told him, "is one of the insects we've developed. A real killer. The Chinese delegation showed much interest in it."

And now, to the right of the first insect, appeared a photo of another.

"This is something even newer," Merlin said. "A strain of insect which has been developed to feed on the other breed you see on the screen."

Eagle's eyebrows furrowed. Neither of the small creatures could be called lovable looking, but the second one, tinted a dark red, had a peculiar shape to its head. Flat and ugly, the antennae were short and curved, as if they were the horns of some demon.

"I don't think I follow you," he said toward the screen. "Why should our people develop a bug to kill another bug which was doing us a service?"

"You follow me precisely, John," Merlin replied. "Our people didn't develop it. The Death Devil is a

47

little invention of the Red Chinese. To be precise, the development of this creature was the main reason for Dr. Yang's group's visit to the United States. They needed samples of our species, needed to see just how they were bred—so that they in turn could breed their killers. The fact that we have this photograph of the thing and the further fact that the killer bugs have begun to show up in several midwestern farming locations—these facts call for immediate countermeasures."

"Can't some kind of DDT or other spray knock them out?"

"Probably, although the creators of this little menace were careful to see that he enters the world with a number of immunities. But, yes, that's being worked on. In the meantime, we've got to be sure that no more of them enter the U.S. I don't suppose I have to explain why."

He didn't. Eagle knew that, for all its industries, the United States—like most societies—still had its economic roots in agriculture. Aside from satisfying the food needs of America's own citizens, the agricultural sector of the American economy provided one of the largest segments of the country's exports. No, there was no need for Merlin to dwell on the complete economic havoc that the ugly little red insect could create.

"We think," the voice from Hawaii was saying, "that the ones we've spotted are among the first to be introduced here. It's no difficult task to bring them into the country, as you can imagine. Therefore, to knock out these bugs, we have to knock out the source—or what we have every reason to believe is the source. We are not all that certain, simply because at the time Dr. Yang wrote his letter, he was not all that certain."

"Dr. Yang? He headed the project, according to what you said."

"That's true, but it wouldn't be the first time a figurehead scientist of great eminence was appointed to lend credibility to a nefarious scheme. It also wouldn't be the first time that the figure of eminence was eliminated once he discovered the true nature of the work he was supposed to be heading. Fortunately for us, Dr. Yang had formed some suspicions before or during his visit here. Fortunately for us also, he put his suspicions on paper—in this letter."

A VuGraph came alive on a screen to the left of where the insects had been. "It's a little long, John, but read it. It contains almost everything we know definitely, the rest being supposition. First, however, you should understand that the letter itself was addressed to the President. It was left with the secretary of the American Entomologist Society with whom Dr. Yang visited while here. His instructions were that the letter should be mailed only in the event of Dr. Yang's death, an event the good doctor made certain that the Society would learn of, in that he initiated several avenues of correspondence—all approved by both sides, of course, since their purpose was exchange of technical information. Thus when the successor of Dr. Yang, this fellow here whose name is Won Chi"—a portion of a group photograph flashed on the screen highlighting a round yellow face—"when Won Chi replied to a letter from an American that, due to Dr. Yang's untimely death, he would in the future be leading the work in China, this letter was sent. It was not mailed, however, but hand-carried to the White House —where as you might imagine it was read with interest."

Eagle's eyes focused on the text:

Dear Mr. President:
    It is my most sincere hope that
this letter will never reach your
eyes, for it will mean that the work

I have been engaged in as well as the
cooperative spirit between our two
countries has been betrayed by those
who do not wish to see any measure
of friendship between us. As I write
this I have a feeling that perhaps
I am being a foolish old man, and yet
there is another feeling within me
which necessitates my writing.

Foolish -- because I have but suspicions and no real knowledge of the
nature of the conspiracy which I
think exists. Trusting therefore that
you will make allowances for the
uncertainties which dominate this
letter, I nonetheless feel it to be
my responsibility to communicate the
following:

It may well be that the work we are
engaged in at our Shih-hsing facilities has as its purpose not merely
the development of a species of
"protector" insects, but something
else. As to what this something else
might be, it has occurred to me that
experimentation with genetic controls
in insects might be applied to larger
species, perhaps even human beings.
I have viewed no work on any species
other than the insect variety, but
this does not mean that there could
not be facilities located elsewhere
which are using our results to further
additional experiments. On the other
hand, it could well be that the results of our work are being used in
the realm of biological warfare of

some kind; that insects are among the
most efficient carriers of natural
and unnatural disease is no secret
to military men in all corners of the
globe we call our world.

In any event, if this letter finds
its way into your hands you will know
that I am no longer among the living.
Further, in all probability, my death
has been "arranged" as a matter of
convenience by those who in reality
are masterminding the real work which
goes on at Shih-hsing and perhaps
elsewhere.

Reality. <u>What is reality</u>? An important question, one answer to which
you will find in the enclosed photograph. The girl's name is Orchid of
Delight. She is my daughter, and she
is on the staff at our facilities.
My one request to you, Mr. President,
is that, should this letter reach
your hands, you arrange to have her
brought from China to the United
States. It will not have eluded you
that she might be of value in giving
firsthand information regarding our
work, but to my mind I am thinking of
her welfare primarily. I wish her
to live in America.

She will be told to expect someone,
but I have enclosed another letter,
this one in Chinese and for her eyes.
She will know by the mark at the
bottom that it has been written in
my hand. She will cooperate, I am sure,
with whomever you send to bring her

from her native land. If he must
identify himself quickly, he should
ask her -- in English -- the question
which I have underlined above. I will
arrange matters so that she understands.

Mr. President, rereading this letter
I feel that perhaps I am a foolish
old man whose senility has overtaken
his mental processes. Yet, because
of my uncertainties, I have put my
thoughts upon paper. I shall not ask
your forgiveness because if I am
wrong only I will know the contents
of what I write.

Respectfully yours,
Yang Kuan-hua

"All right," Eagle said. "I've read it. How about the
other letter—the one in Chinese?"

"Very brief. Mostly a statement of his belief that it is
in her best interest to leave China."

As Eagle nodded, the letter disappeared. In its place
was a map of the People's Republic of China. To the
left of that was a photograph of a girl.

Eagle's attention did not return to the map until the
girl's picture faded. Merlin obviously was watching
the focus of his employee's eyes. "Charming girl, yes?"
the old man said with a laugh. "But remember, John,
she's Chinese, she's communist, and thus she could be
deadly."

"I take it we're going in after her."

"You take it correct. Although we now know what
the secret project is, we don't know the location of the
additional breeding grounds. The girl may know—
especially if she knows or suspects that her father was
murdered. Your job is to destroy the Shih-hsing facili-

ties and bring the girl and her knowledge out with you."

Eagle was thoughtful for a moment. "You seem absolutely certain that there are additional breeding grounds."

"Not absolutely, no. But we suspect it strongly. A matter of efficiency, John. Unless some method were used to freeze the Death Devils alive, they'd never make the trip from China to the U.S. They have a very short lifespan."

"In which case—"

"In which case, yes, the place of breeding probably is somewhere close to us. Certainly in the Western Hemisphere. Which is another cause for concern. If something should go wrong at the breeding grounds, and if enough of the insects should escape, uncontrolled . . ."

He did not complete the sentence.

He didn't have to.

A red grease-pencil marked an X on a portion of the China map. Under that map two additional maps came into view. One showed the terrain around the village of Shih-hsing. The main feature of the second was a railroad running from Hong Kong to Canton. And now another photograph was flashed before Eagle.

"The man you are looking at is a chemicals expert, John. His name is Cyril Compton."

CHAPTER 6

When the brakes began to screech, Eagle was ready. His crouched position made it easy to transfer the weight of his body to his palms. As soon as that had been accomplished, however, he was moving—fast.

It takes a bit of time to slow a fast-moving train to a complete halt. Eagle had no intention of waiting. The area on both sides of the tracks would soon be swarming with green uniforms and rifles, but the Chinese would wait until the train was moving at what was at least a crawl. Eagle, on the other hand—

He moved rapidly to the front of the car, then took the distance between that and the one before it at a leap, the *thud* of his boots probably not even heard below him, such was the noise of brakes on wheels. Still he ran forward until he came to the front end of the car.

Now.

The train continued to slow, the swiftness with which the landscape slipped by slackening by small degrees. The attaché case belted snugly to his back and his pistol in his belt, Eagle swung down from the top and onto the platform, taking extreme care that the boot-

54

end of his swing neatly connected—toe to throat—with the Chinese guard who stood below, rifle in hand. The second rifleman—on the opposite platform—hadn't gotten his weapon up to shoulder height before Eagle leaped over the rail.

He took the hard-packed earth on his right shoulder, rolling over onto his hip and then rolling over again. The attaché case made for an awkward landing, but that couldn't be helped. The pistol had jerked free and Eagle's first movement after coming to a rest was a swift retreat to regain it. It was no more than a dozen feet away, but that proved to be too far.

The bullet which spattered the dirt between himself and the pistol made that abundantly clear.

Eagle flattened and rolled, then jumped up to a crouch. Farther up along the tracks, the train had come to a complete halt. Only one green uniform was out on the turf, probably the rifleman he'd surprised on the platform. That one now was taking another bead on Eagle. It would be only a matter of instants before he'd have company—and plenty of it.

It was time to leave the party, with the Tokarev or without it.

The countryside along this stretch of track was a series of ridges, sharp crevices intermingled with small valleys, the overall effect of which was to resemble some kind of farm terracing gone wild, or the kind of trenches used in World War I set one next to the other. It looked like a greatly magnified fingerprint, in fact, a print taken from a man's hand which had seen rough and heavy work. Or so Merlin had said when they'd viewed blow-up photographs of the area.

Eagle, however, preferred the trench analogy, because that was how he viewed the protective feature of the first one as he dove over its lip, two bullets ricocheting from the ground around him. There were more shots now as Eagle, crouched low, began running in the direction from which the train had come. For the count of seven he ran—lucky number seven it had better be!—then leaped up and over into the next trench, his feet running as soon as they touched the bottom of the gully.

Seven again, then jump, then run, the thuds of bullets sounding like the Anvil Chorus. But that was all to the good. Riflemen firing are not riflemen running, by definition. And from the sound of the shouts of the men behind him and to the right, he was making good distance.

Up and over and into the next valley. Ten paces this time, then up and over again. Three shots the first time, four the second. Eagle decided. It was time to begin *Operation Massage Parlor.*

He stopped running. In an instant he was out of his jacket and boots, both of which landed in different places along the floor of the gully. It wasn't a time for neatness; speed was the only requirement. The fastest time the previous evening had been eighteen seconds, but he recognized that now, even with the pressure of necessity upon him, he was going to beat that time. Because now he didn't have to be careful about buttons getting yanked off—or the zipper he realized he'd just extended to the level of his knees—no, this time he would qualify for the *Guinness Book of World Records,* if in fact they had a category called "undressing" or "disrobing." But then, of course, he'd have to have somebody around to attest to his victory, and no one was available. Pity. Like hell—he didn't want anybody around.

Pity.

Somebody was. Not right there, but getting too close for comfort.

His ears picked up the sound, a strange one. He didn't realize what it was until he remembered something he'd read about the Chinese. It was a piece in *The New York Times* in which some Chinese diplomat or other had commented upon what currently was called America's energy crisis. "We do not have such a thing in our land. That is because we do not have the mixed blessings of so many automobiles. Most Chinese travel either on foot or by bicycle."

It was a bicycle that Eagle's ears heard now.

A bicycle. No, two. Funny that Merlin hadn't mentioned that there might be a couple of them on the train. *Not* funny that right now, in the very gully in which a naked Expeditor stood staring toward the bend in the gully northward, that two of those two-wheeled contraptions were coming directly toward him unseen, but not for long.

The naked John Eagle looked at the naked John Eagle and laughed. It wasn't a naked Eagle he saw at all. The false plastic pot-belly betrayed him. He was a naked Cyril Compton. A chemical salesman.

Very well. If our good Chinese hosts can't wait to see our samples . . .

Swiftly now he opened the attaché case and located one of the little clear plastiglass vials. Purple was the color of the fluid. Not good enough. He located one which was green in color, then another. Both caps were twisted sharply to the right. This was the on-impact setting. Now all that awaited was the coming of the target.

The little man in the lead nearly upset his bike when, upon rounding the bend, he saw the naked white man some ten yards farther on, a man who was cocking back his arm as if to throw something. He turned to the man on the second bicycle to shout out some order. The order was neither shouted nor heard. Only the bright orange explosion which kicked up mounds of dirt—and pieces of two bikes and their Chinese riders.

Instantly there was a second explosion—this one several gullies closer to the train tracks. Eagle grinned at the confused shouts, none of which sounded at all close to him. That would give them something to think about. In the meantime . . .

Swiftly he used the single-edged blade from his safety razor to slit the side of the attaché case. Pulling the flat plastic bundle from inside the surface rent, he opened the package. It was in two parts, identical in size. One part he set aside for the moment; he wouldn't have a need for that for at least a couple of days. But the first . . .

It was a suit of plastic, complete with a hood and face mask and gloves and boots. All in one piece, all of which when on a man's body stretched to fit like a second skin, the suit had several properties. It was bullet-proof, for one thing. For another, it was climatically adaptable, keeping the wearer's body temperature normal regardless of the extremities of cold or heat which surrounded him.

A third thing about the suit:

It was difficult as hell to put on in a hurry.

He had both legs and his left arm into the thing when his ears heard another bike. Deftly he bent down and picked up another green-colored vial, twisting the white cap to the right and placing the device between his teeth. Into the empty sleeve went his right arm, Eagle's fingers moving snugly into the glove, then the plastic zipper moved upward to just under his chin. Now all there was left was the hood and face mask. They went on none too swiftly.

There was just one more little chore. Unfortunately, Eagle heard the bike stop, heard feet step from the pedals and onto solid earth. Roughly about fifteen yards to the north—but in the gully to his right. Just over the ridge, where the rising yellow face—

58

The Chinese cried in triumph, his pistol barking twice.

He was a lousy marksman, one of his bullets missing his target by a good six feet. The other, however, slapped Eagle's thigh. The Chinese looked with almost round eyes at the man he'd just shot. He was trying to sort out just what had happened when the little green vial dropped near his left foot.

Then he blew up.

Eagle's hands were busy before the orange sun faded from the landscape, busy at the back of his left knee. The suit had one additional property, one the Expeditor had found very helpful in the past. In a small pocket to the rear of the knee there was a thing called a chameleon unit. Only once had the device failed him, and that had been after he'd crashed through a high-voltage electric fence. But failure of any kind was something Merlin would not tolerate and, therefore, the unit had gone back to the drawing board. The model Eagle now plugged into place was impervious to electrical attack. What's more, it would perform its primary function as well as its predecessors, that function being to change the coloration of the suit so as to blend into any landscape. It was not true invisibility —there would still be the danger of shadows and a full silhouette when the wearer of the suit and an observer were positioned correctly with respect to a strong light source—but it was the next best thing.

One further improvement had been made in the unit. It was smaller than its predecessor, the new one being about the size of a ten-cent piece.

He connected the wires. Then listening to the sounds around him, he crouched over the attaché case. There were twenty of the vials left now, most of them green but some purple. These he quietly placed into several pockets which were located throughout the plastic suit material. Then he took the other plastic packet which had come from the case and attached it to a place at the small of his back. As he did, that too changed to an earthy color, having been connected to the chameleon unit.

He stepped back from the case. He was ready to move out.

Except that he wasn't. Merlin, after all, had said it himself:

"Phase Three not only is composed of your escape from the train, John, but it's also necessary that you put on a bit of a show. You've got to raise so much havoc that the powers that be will have to track down just who the destroyer is. Only then can we be sure they'll search for and find Compton's card. Only then will they thoroughly quiz all the train guards and find out—perhaps through torture—that you spoke Russian to one of them. And only then will they bother to confirm the fact that Compton also heard you speak Russian."

"And how do they confirm that?" Eagle had asked.

"They will learn that from their man who works at the American Consulate in Hong Kong. He's a bit of a double agent, but he doesn't think either side knows it. As far as I know, neither side does. But I do."

Eagle had not understood all this. "But, sir—you told me to be sure to tell him that he was *not* to go to our consulate."

"Of course. I also told you to tell him that the consulate would be searching for him. That will scare him plenty. Plus the fact, the man will have no passport and no money. Where else would he possibly go? If fear doesn't drive him to the U.S. Consulate, then necessity will."

"I feel sorry for Mr. Cyril Compton."

Merlin's voice turned serious. "So do I, John, but there come times when many people are called to serve their countries. Wartimes, especially. Mr. Cyril Compton doesn't know it, but this is a time of war, and he is about to serve. It will be a bit unpleasant, but he at least is not up there on the front line."

"He may think so for a while," Eagle had commented.

"I hope so, John. And he will—if you really give them a good show."

A good show.

He'd killed four of them on the train. He'd detonated three vial-grenades and killed three men that he knew of and maybe more if he'd been lucky with the one he'd thrown wild. Did that qualify as being "a good show"?

Probably, but this aspect of the operation was more in the realm of public relations, and that was something Eagle knew very little about. It would pay to make sure *everybody* agreed it was a good show.

He moved up the gully, back toward the train. Already his Apache-trained ears had heard the movement of several pairs of boots coming along it toward him.

The lead rifleman rounded the corner slowly, carefully. The man they were after had explosives, after all, and while there was no certainty that he was around this particular corner in this particular gully, there was no certainty that he wasn't, either. He himself had argued some five minutes ago that they were foolish to be in the gullies, that they should walk the ridges instead, allowing them to see down into several of the valleys at once. But the sergeant had been smarter. "Excellent suggestion—excellent!" he'd said. "Much easier then for our fugitive to find targets for his weapons. Such a nice tall silhouette you would make too. I assume you are volunteering for this suicide mission?"

He had shaken his head, duly complimenting the

sergeant on his perceptiveness. The sergeant, on his part, had merely sneered. "That, soldier, is why I am a sergeant and why you are what you are. Move!"

He had moved, but cautiously, the lead man of a string of six, all of them except the last carrying rifles. The last carried a pistol, but then he was the sergeant. Yes, there had been something to what the sergeant had said. Sergeants rarely had to be the lead man. In all the mock exercises he had been through it was always the same. Obviously the problem for any soldier was to live long enough to be a sergeant. Then, when the crunch came, you would continue to live—while the underlings went first to get their insides shot out.

Shot? No, not in this case. The fugitive had bombs.

That, however, was not a comforting thought.

Carefully . . . very carefully. . . .

His eyes scanned the distance between this turn and the next with close attention to detail. It was obvious to him at first glance that there was no one—no person—before him. But that didn't mean that there was no explosive device. Something lying on the earth, or buried halfway under it, something if stepped upon—

The soldier behind him nudged him with his rifle. He sneered back at the man and the four others who seemed impatient to get him killed.

The capitalist bastards! Only they would have this sophisticated kind of weaponry. They or the Russian revisionists! Yes, the lieutenant who had been attacked in the water closet—a thing which would have been very funny if he had not been a lieutenant and in command of all of them—he had said that. The man had spoken in Russian. But these days, what was the difference? Capitalist, imperialist, Russian communist? The Chinese soldier had been trained to hate all of them, to kill all of them. They said now—*they,* the speakers for the leaders who lived far north in Peking—

that the Americans were their friends now. That would be all right, and it was. After all, no one had had to fight with an American, anyway. But only a few years ago he had sat in classrooms learning about what fat pigs the Americans were. Had the Americans gotten less fat? Or was it instead that fatness in itself was something the People's Republic no longer cared about when choosing its friends and enemies?

And how in Mao's name was a common soldier to know?

Answer: he wasn't. He just did his duty. And duty was whatever was defined for him by his immediate superior. In this case, the sergeant behind him, the sergeant who was in fact defining that duty at that moment.

"Move on—there's no one ahead, nothing."

The soldier swallowed heavily and stepped out.

The sergeant was wrong.

In the shadow of the gully wall to his right side, something moved. Then something seemed to grasp his arms—and lift him upward inches from the ground and turn him so that once again he faced the party he had been leading. He shouted out his protest, just as the other men began shouting too. And then a very strange thing happened.

His rifle fired.

His rifle fired!

The soldier nearest him crashed backward into the others, a bloodied hole in his forehead. With wild eyes the sergeant was screaming as, mysteriously, the tightly held rifle spoke again—and a second soldier dropped.

"I'm not doing this!" the rifleman shrieked. "Believe me—"

But it was evident that they didn't believe him. The remaining guns—two rifles and the sergeant's pistol—

63

open fired a point-blank range, cutting off the man's protest and final breath in the same instant.

Dropping the dead Chinese, the perfectly camouflaged Expeditor lunged at the three standing men. Simultaneously the edge of his right hand dealt a death blow to the temple of one of the riflemen and his left heel unhinged the jaw of the second. The sergeant with the pistol screamed and turned to run. His boots hit the ground four times before he felt a sudden pressure slam into his back. The snap of his spine made a loud crack but it is doubtful that his brain registered the sound before sudden death overtook it.

Eagle picked up the pistol, a Tokarev to replace the one he'd lost. The sergeant had three extra clips of ammunition on his belt which Eagle placed into the left-bicep pocket of his suit. He looked at the corpses. Six of them. Six more. Added to seven that made thirteen. Did that add up to a good show?

Maybe, but it was an unlucky number.

He climbed to the lip of the gully. He had thought that the screaming and shooting would attract the attention of other soldiers and he had been right. They were swarming toward him like bees toward honey.

Excellent, but this time it was the bees who were going to get stung.

Three of them did, in rapid-fire succession, then the weapon clicked empty.

Eagle considered using one of the three clips in his suit. He unzipped the pocket and slammed the clip home, then decided. No. The total now was sixteen. Sweet sixteen. That ought to be "show" enough, even for Merlin.

He placed the weapon in the tight space between his back and the plastic bundle which he had attached there, then he slid down to the bottom of the gully and began a long-striding loping run. He pulled the mask from his face so that he could take the deep breaths which would fill his lungs with the oxygen which in turn would feed his sleek musculature. He ran eastward, but soon he would turn north and head in that direction. He had studied the terrain well in the briefing room of Camp Three, and he knew there were several options open to him. He did not have to run the entire hundred and forty miles which separated himself and his target. But even with the intervening land features, he knew that if he wanted to do it all on foot he could make it easily in three full days, perhaps in two and a half. As a youth he had learned the secret of running for long hours over long distances, and as an Expeditor the knowledge and ability had come in very handy.

But he didn't have to make detailed plans now. Phase Three was completed and he was free of the train, free in Red China. Running free.

With the fingers of his right hand he folded down a flap of material at his left wrist. Flat under where the flap had been was a strip of plastic of a somewhat thicker but still malleable substance. It was called a "strip-watch" by its developer, its three hands keeping time at exact standards. A compass and signaling device as well, its dial had been set at local time days previous when the suit had been packed in the special attaché case. The time now was three-thirty.

Three-thirty and all was well.

Sixteen deaths—at least—behind him; it felt good to be running free. It felt good, for the time being, that he had no strict schedule to follow, that he could take whatever time he desired to reach the girl whose father said would be expecting him.

If, however, he somehow could have perceived the thoughts of that girl at that moment, he might not have been so complacent.

CHAPTER 7

She looked across her desk with an attempt at compassion for the man who stood there. Won Chi, after all, was now in charge of the project, and that made him worthy of her respect—or at least the motions of respect. But here he was, just as if her father had been alive, as if he were appealing to her to intercede on his behalf.

"They cannot do it!" he cried, almost as if he were a baby.

"I fail to see—" she began, but was immediately cut off.

"They're moving the larvae—the special ones. Without even consulting me. *Me!* Am I not the project leader?"

She smiled. "Yes. You are the project leader."

Evidently the fat man caught a tone of displeasure in her answer.

"I am sorry. I beg your pardon. By my referring to my position, I did not mean any slight to your inestimable father, but—"

"But you are project leader," she completed. "If that

is so, why do you come to me? I no longer have influence with the project leader."

He paused. "I wish not to offend yourself, but it would appear that your influence is not as small as you would have me believe."

Her voice was cold. "Won Chi, have I been promoted to some elevated position—without my knowledge? I hardly believe that can be the case."

He shook his head. "You misunderstand me."

"And you, Won Chi—you are not making yourself clear."

"Perhaps not." Beads of perspiration were breaking out on his forehead. The man obviously was very uncomfortable. "Perhaps not. But I have been led to believe that you do have influence with certain people of power, who—"

"An excellent question, Won Chi."

"Question?"

"Yes. Who? Who is it with whom I am supposed to have such a measure of influence that it should bring you here to me this afternoon? Who?"

"Colonel Chou." He said it quietly almost as if whispering. The focus of his eyes moved to some point on the top of her desk. He stood motionless. Waiting.

At last she repeated, "Colonel Chou. May I ask why you suppose me to have a special influence upon this person?"

He did not answer. She knew he would not.

"I see," she said. "I do not admit to having any special influence, but . . ."

His eyes lifted hopefully. She smiled.

"But—I will listen to your complaint. Is that agreeable to you?"

Won Chi could not restrain himself. "He has ordered the removal of the larvae!"

"You have said that earlier."

"But to *where?* And *why?* All our experimental evidence tells us that this is the best location for testing. The climatological evidence, as you may know—"

"Perhaps Miss Yang does *not* know."

Won Chi's face turned pale as he craned his neck around to view the newcomer to Miss Yang's office. "Sir, I—"

"You did not knock, Colonel Chou," the girl said.

The uniformed man bowed to the woman, but his eyes still remained upon the white-coated fat man. "My pardons. Often, in my desire to accomplish my tasks swiftly, I do not always observe the correct forms of conduct. I trust you will forgive me."

Orchid inclined her forehead slightly. "You have not offended me, Colonel. It was, after all, not myself whom you interrupted."

There was a flash of something in the thin military man's eyes. Something which reminded the girl of lightning—if in fact there were anything such as *black* lightning. But it was momentary. He smiled.

"Far be it from anything in my mind to interrupt the project leader's words." He looked intensely at Won Chi. "Please continue."

"I was saying nothing of importance, Colonel," the fat man said.

The colonel grinned. "I see. You fellow scientists have your little secrets, I assume."

Won Chi's face almost collapsed. "No—no, sir. It's not that. All I was saying—"

"It is of no importance," the Colonel said smugly. "The reason I came here was that I was told you might be here, Won Chi. I would like to speak with you about certain new arrangements I have made. In my office. In thirty minutes. Will that be all right?"

"Yes, sir."

"It will give you sufficient time to complete your business with Miss Yang?"

"Yes, sir."

"Excellent. Good day, Miss Yang."

His exit line delivered, the thin colonel took his leave. When he closed the door behind him, the fat man in the white coat looked as if he were about to faint.

"I trust you have no further business with me, Won Chi," the girl said levelly. "It would appear that you are about to be consulted after all. In thirty minutes, in the Colonel's office, if I heard the colonel correctly."

"Miss Yang—"

"Please. The administration of this project is not my affair. It has never been my affair, even when my father headed the installation and what took place within it. I am a technician, trying to do my assigned job. That was the case while my father was alive, and it is the case now. Do you, as project head, have any fault to find in my work?"

"No—of course not, no!"

"Then I would appreciate being allowed to get on with that work. Unless you have something further to discuss with me."

He took a sheepish step backward. "No, there is . . . nothing."

She smiled. "You say they are moving the larvae? Which larvae? All of them?"

He looked at her with undecided eyes. "Not—not all. No, not all."

"Which, then?"

"I—Miss Yang, I'm sorry to have disturbed you. You are not familiar with all aspects of this project, and there are reasons for that. There are certain aspects which are closely held to but a very few of us."

She nodded. "A few. And do you not think that as the daughter of the man who was the project head, that I might now know about these—as you call them— certain aspects?"

The look on his face told her what she wanted to

know. It was a look of fear, of realizing that he might have said too much, gone too far. When he left the office, when she was alone, she made her decision.

Her watch told her she had slightly more than twenty-five minutes to prepare. Won Chi and the colonel were going to talk, but there would be a third pair of ears listening.

"Colonel—" Through the closed door of Colonel Chou's office the voices which reached the girl's ears were muffled, but for the most part audible. As she sat in the outer office, she was glad that it was empty aside from herself. Originally the outer office had been designed for a secretary or an assistant, but Colonel Chou was proud of the fact that it was not occupied. "The Republic is not yet so wealthy that I feel I can afford such a luxury," he had declared to the staff, neglecting to mention that he had a host of uniformed runners waiting for but the snap of his fingers to jump to do his bidding.

Won Chi's voice seemed to whine. While the colonel's was as cold as ice.

"I do not think you understand, Won Chi. The larvae have been moved because I felt it was dangerous to keep the strain here."

"But, Colonel, they were developing nicely. I assure you that I had taken every precaution—"

"I am speaking not so much of a danger of the process going wrong."

"Ah! You mean a *security* danger! But even so, there are very few of us who know the true nature of the special strain. I should think there would be no fear of having an agent of another country infiltrate—"

"It is not an agent of another country I was concerned about, Doctor. You see, the project has entered a new phase. The larvae have been taken to—"

And here there came a word the girl did not hear

clearly. Something like *Chirkee* or *Chickee.* Won Chi, however, recognized the word, which obviously was a place name—and he sounded totally surprised:

"We are *attacking?* But that was not supposed to be! The special strain was developed only as a possible defensive—"

"Silence!"

"But it is true. You have said so yourself, many times, that the orders you have received clearly—"

Colonel Chou's laugh cut him off. "Perhaps they do, Doctor. And perhaps I have made some decisions of my own as to how the little insects you have so kindly developed for us should be used. Sometimes, Won Chi, our leaders do not always know what is best for our people. Nonetheless, I have been authorized to move samples of the strain to *Chirkee"*—that's what it sounded like, although the girl knew of no such place name—"and I have operated completely within that authority."

"Samples, yes! But the *entire* strain—"

"Wait!"

The girl suddenly rose, something in the colonel's command alerting her, warning her—

She was out of the office and around the corner in the corridor when she heard Colonel Chou's door open. She stopped her motion, holding her breathing still. The door closed. Still she did not move, not until she was sure there was no one coming toward her.

Quietly, she left the building.

It was nine o'clock that evening when, from somewhere outside her own dormitory, she heard someone cry out. She recognized the voice, or imagined she did. She strongly suspected she would never see Dr. Won Chi again.

It was eight in the morning in Washington, a fact Merlin did not comment upon *per se,* but there was a

71

definite touch of sarcasm in his voice as he accepted the black telephone from Polly.

"Good morning, Mr. Secretary. We taxpayers take a measure of satisfaction to see that our civil servants are active at such an early hour."

"Er, yes," the secretary said. "I suppose it is a bit early out there where you are."

"Three in the morning. Two minutes after three, to be exact."

"All right, Merlin—I'm sorry if I awakened you."

"You didn't. The late show on TV was marvelous." Not that he'd been watching anything so trivial. He had in fact been listening to a number of telephone calls. He also had known to expect a call from the man who at the moment was on the other end of the line. "I don't suspect you'd like to hear about it. The TV show, I mean."

"Hong Kong," the secretary said. His voice was flat, as if his mind was weary.

"A lovely city," Merlin replied. "A bit crowded, but—"

"Damn you, Merlin—stop jousting with me! I want a straight answer. Was it your man in Hong Kong or not?"

Sitting in his wheelchair, Merlin accepted the warmed snifter of brandy from Polly, winking at her. "My man in Hong Kong? Which man would that be, Mr. Secretary? I have a couple of men in Hong Kong. They too complain about the crowded conditions—and the cost of living as well. It's really skyrocketed recently, as you may or may not know."

There was a pause. "Are you through toying with me, Merlin?"

"Yes, Mr. Secretary. I believe my old ego—my *warhorse* ego, I believe you once called it—has been satisfied. What would you like to know?"

"A Mr. Cyril Compton—does the name ring a bell?"

"One, yes."

"A loud one?"

"Like a cymbal."

A rush of air into the phone. And then, quietly, "I thought so. Merlin, do you realize what you've done?"

Merlin smiled. "I understand perfectly what I've done. Now, perhaps, you'd like to tell me what it is *you* think I've done."

"All right, Merlin—from the top. At noon Hong Kong time Mr. Cyril Compton awakens in his hotel room and stumbles out of the clothes closet where *for some reason* he has been sleeping through the night. Feeling the effects of some kind of drug, he is not totally aware of his physical condition—he is, I should add, totally naked. He therefore somewhat startles the cleaning maid who is attempting to make his bed. No, *startles* is not the precise word, not strong enough— especially since Mr. Compton, in his frantic exit from the closet and entry into the room proper, stumbles over something and collides with said maid, driving the two of them onto the yet-unmade bed."

"I always prefer that sort of thing in the morning myself," Merlin said.

The secretary coughed abrasively. "Not so our cleaning maid, however, who by the way seems to have been spending most of her free time watching a good many low-budget *kung-fu* movies. She dealt our Mr. Compton several effective chops and kicks before she rediscovered her feminism and ran from the room screaming like a banshee."

Merlin laughed. "That must have been quite a sight."

"Quite, but no more so than Mr. Compton's chasing her down the hall, shouting that she'd probably given him a double hernia—or worse. Nonetheless, things soon quieted down when Mr. Compton was jumped by three or more persons, a mixture of hotel staff and concerned guests, and whisked to a neutral corner, which in this instance was a broom closet. Ten minutes later, a representative of the Consulate General's office was on the scene."

"In the broom closet?"

"Don't be funny, Merlin." Another pause. "By the way, have you heard anything of these particular events before my telling you?"

"Blow by blow, word for word. Almost. You tell it with greater dramatic impact, if I might say so."

"Merlin—was it your man, Eagle? I want a straight answer."

"Straight answer: Yes."

"Good God, Merlin! You—"

"I, to interrupt, was asked to handle a somewhat delicate matter. I—with Eagle—am handling that matter."

"Yes, but the Chinese—"

"The *Red* Chinese, Mr. Secretary."

"All right. The Red Chinese. They are screaming about a man looking like Compton and having Compton's papers having killed God knows how many people on their side of the border."

"But they don't figure this killer to be American, do they, Mr. Secretary?"

"*No!* But, Lord, man—the Russians are screaming, too. They know *they* didn't have a hand in this!"

"Bullroar," Merlin said. "The Russians never know what each and every one of their wings is doing. They can't be sure about anything."

"Just like us, you mean. That was what you were going to add, wasn't it?"

"I take it," Merlin said pleasantly, "that you've heard also from our intelligence people—or yours."

74

"You're damned right I have. Merlin, your man just can't go around doing as he pleases—"

"He does as *I* please," Merlin said softly. "It happens to be explicitly spelled out in his contract."

"But—but why, Merlin? Why did you have to go this route of implicating the Russians?"

"Because, Mr. Secretary, John Eagle had to get inside Red China. He had to do so in a way that would not endanger all your delicate relations with Red China. Thus, he could not appear to be an American. If not American, then what? Russian sounded very good to my mind."

"But, Merlin, we've got some delicate relations with the Russians too."

Merlin frowned. "I've had some, myself. But, as you are fond of saying, I'm just an old war-horse. If you don't like the way I do things, next time call on somebody else."

"Merlin—"

"It's late, Mr. Secretary. I should say that it's late here. Unless you have anything pertinent to discuss . . ." His voice trailed off, waiting.

The secretary's voice was like steel. "One day, Merlin—"

"One day, Mr. Secretary, I'll be dead as hell. I suppose that the security of the United States of America will be improved a thousand percent by that event."

"No, Merlin, it won't—"

Merlin laughed sharply. "You're goddamned right it won't."

Polly Perkins smiled at her employer. "Should you really have hung up on him?"

He smiled back, handing her the brandy snifter for a refill. "Polly, after that beautiful made-to-order exit line, all else would have been anti-climax."

CHAPTER 8

It was dark when Eagle skirted the western edge of the village of Tung-kuan and quietly approached the river labeled Tung on the map he had memorized. He did not feel tired, not at all, but he had been longing to reach the water, for only the water would relieve him of a burden which was not all that heavy, but which did not allow his body to behave at its maximum functioning.

The trappings of Cyril Compton. Now they could be removed.

The plastic substance he had used to mold his features and his protruding stomach was tough stuff, but it could be shed easily by immersion in water. Merlin's lab people were aware of the fact that a disguise which was water-soluble might not be among the best of disguises, so they had taken the necessary precautions in its devising. Thus, even in the steadiest downpour of rain—as long as there were instants of plain old air reaching his face—the disguise would hold. "But don't take any baths, Mr. Eagle," Merlin's chemist had told him. "Cleanliness may well be next to godliness, but in this instance it would pay you to opt for a less saintly life. For the time you wish your disguise in place, that is."

Well, that time had passed and, although the plastic suit had kept his body cool, the appendages of Compton-likeness had caused their minor discomforts.

Quietly he slipped into the water, first making sure that the Tokarev was safe and secure in a watertight pocket under his left arm. He stroked out silently, his movements barely disturbing the surface of the water. Then, when he was satisfied that he was far enough from sight of land, he unzipped the front of the suit and removed the face mask and hood.

The entire process took less than three minutes. The tough plastic melted from him as if it were ice under a slow-burning torch. Even the mustache appeared to melt, although when he applied it the previous night he had supposed it to be comprised of some kind of animal hair. A moot question, one which had absolutely no concern to him now, not even a mild curiosity. He checked to be sure no vestige of the plastic remained, then he rolled over onto his stomach and headed for the bank opposite to the one he'd left. He'd be having his chance to do some real swimming later, perhaps tomorrow afternoon or evening. In the meantime, his current task was to get the Tung River behind him.

From where Eagle had left the train one could draw a straight line to the village of Shih-hsing, the line being almost due north. The Tung River unfortunately separated this line, close to its origin, on an almost perfect east-west course. Although it curved northward eventually, the eventually was too eventual. Thus the river had to be crossed. However, once that was done, all there was between Eagle and his objective was a goodly amount of land. Rugged land.

Therefore, he did not intend to follow the straight-line route. Instead, he had two options, both of which led him on a northwest course for some seventy miles until he reached a tributary, the River Hsi. There he would have a choice, depending either upon the level of river traffic going up this northeasterly bound waterway or upon his whim. In any case, the Hsi tributary ended some eighty miles from target, which would mean further advancement by land. Again, rough land.

His other alternative was to cross the Hsi, then move in a northwest line for some forty miles to the Pei River. A major waterway in this area of China, its northeasterly course, almost parallel to the Hsi, would bring him directly to a point within less than ten miles from Shih-hsing.

There was also a third alternative. If he wished, he could follow the Hsi tributary to any point he chose, then cross to the Pei to resume his waterway journey. But as he now slowed his stroke to a quiet approach to the shoreline of the Tung, he wasn't about to make up his mind. There was, after all, no possibility to assess what he had not yet seen with his own eyes.

Someone will be coming. Someone—

She had not been dreaming, although it was past the time she normally went to sleep. Lying on the top of her bed on her back, she realized that she still wore her laboratory coat, which under the circumstances was good. For the sound which had stopped her—well, imagining, yes—was a quiet rap upon the door of her room.

The quiet rap became louder with repetition.

"Who is there?" she asked.

"It is I, Colonel Chou." She had not needed the name. The voice of the man could not be mistaken for another.

"It is late, Colonel."

"Very late," he said with a gravity that told her he was not talking just about the hour of the night. "I

78

must talk with you, Miss Yang. Please, open the door."

Swiftly she considered her alternatives. Just as swiftly, she determined that she had none. She rose from the bed and stepped to the door, fixing her hair as she did. *What, little Orchid—you fix your hair for this murderer of your own flesh and blood?*

She almost staggered from the question her own mind shot to her, then she smiled with determination. *Yes. I fix my hair, and I will smile toward Colonel Chou. And I swear by the stars in the sky that I will see this man dead at my feet!*

"Colonel Chou," she said as she opened the door. "I am sorry that I did not respond sooner to your knocking. I was—"

"Asleep, of course," he said, taking her hand—taking it, but not noticing the sudden shudder of her shoulders. Or not seeming to notice. The girl whose name was Orchid of Delight suddenly felt her spine grow cold. A man of his supposed talents at ferreting out the hidden feelings of others could not possibly miss—

But, no, he *didn't* seem to notice. He was either a very good actor—an excellent possibility—or, more likely, when those feelings concerned himself, he was a supreme egotist. The girl suspected that the latter was the case.

"Asleep," he repeated. "I recognize that the timing of my visit is not the best, but it is a matter of some urgency which brings me to your room, Miss Yang."

"I did not doubt that to be the case, Colonel. How can I be of assistance to you?"

She did not like the flicker of excitement which brightened his eyes, but it was momentary.

"Miss Yang, I wish you to consider the position of head of this project, following in the work of your noble father."

79

She looked at him steadily. "But, Colonel—Dr. Won Chi—"

"Is no longer a factor. He has been—ah, transferred. Yes, transferred."

"That seems rather sudden," she said, not now able to look at him. "Only today, he—"

"Sudden, yes," the Colonel broke in. "He was needed elsewhere. Such are the difficulties of our country, Miss Yang. We have so much worthwhile work to be accomplished, yet at the same time we do not have the requisite number of properly trained minds to carry out that work." He smiled. "Well, what do you say? Do you accept the position?"

She stepped backward one step. "Colonel, you have asked me to *consider* accepting the position. I hardly have had time even to digest the fact that Dr. Won Chi no longer is with us."

A bad statement? Had that been put the wrong way? No, he didn't blink an eyelash.

"I can understand that, Miss Yang, but time is of the utmost importance. Very shortly, we will be dismantling this location."

"Dismantling—"

"Yes. It is being moved elsewhere for—ah—climatic reasons. Yes, climatic reasons. I was hoping that you would—"

"Pardon, Colonel, but where is the project being moved to? I was not aware that—"

"No. None of the people here—or very few, at least—are aware of the necessity to shift our base of operations. As to the precise location, I am sorry that that information cannot be divulged at this time. In due course, however, if you accept this task which the People's Republic—"

"I have always accepted the tasks asked of me," she said, allowing her voice to come through with a slight chill. She was inwardly glad that he had given her the opportunity to vent even a little slice of her pent-up wrath, and he in turn fortunately misjudged the reason for it.

He sighed. "Yes, you always have been a loyal citizen, Miss Yang. I, after all, have access to those records which prove that without doubt. But, as to this position—"

"There are others far more deserving than myself."

"Let me be the judge of that."

She shook her head, being careful to smile as she did so. "I'm afraid that, in this matter, you are not the most competent judge. This is a matter of scientific knowledge, one in which I have a measure of competence. And, in my opinion—"

"I have offered you the job, Miss Yang. I might add that, if you do not accept it, my report must be—well, at the least it must be somewhat unfavorable. Then, too, I ask you to remember two additional things. First, that with the dismantling of these facilities you will have no effective job."

"When will that take place?"

"Three days from now. Three."

She nodded. "You mentioned two things to remember. The second?"

He bowed slightly. "The second thing I wish you to remember—or, I should say, ponder upon—is that I will be relocating to the new location. I should very much like to have your company. I think you and I could—well, work very well in tandem together."

"I—I have no reason to believe otherwise, Colonel. Your professional demeanor always has been of the highest—"

"I was not speaking only of our professionalism, Miss Yang. I suspect that you are aware of that fact."

"I am, as always, flattered, Colonel Chou."

81

"But?"

She smiled at him more fully, even as her heart pounded to the extent that she was certain his ears must hear it. "I did not mention a *but,* Colonel. It is merely that I must—as you yourself said—*consider* this weighty matter. My skills—"

"Are sufficient, I am sure. After all, you were your father's closest confidante, were you not?"

A warning bell rang somewhere in the back of her mind. What did he mean by that? No matter, she could not afford to hesitate in replying, could not afford to sift through the several levels of possible meaning his question-statement might contain.

"He told me much about some things, little about others. He informed me as he saw fit, I would say."

The thin man smiled at the response, perhaps recognizing the fact that it communicated absolutely nothing, the girl thought. But the smile seemed genuine, if Colonel Chou was capable of expressing any emotion genuinely. *Pain, perhaps. Yes, maybe pain. And maybe I will be privileged to see that expression— directly before his inevitable death!*

"Miss Yang, I know I have said this before to you, but still I feel that your father did not especially like me, that he may have spoken ill of me in your presence."

She shook her head. "Colonel, I do not know what gives you that idea. While it is true that my father had little patience for people who did not think in scientific modes of thought, he did not harbor ill will toward non-scientists on that account. Certainly, he did not express any opinion—not to his daughter, at least— that you were anything other than what I know you to be."

Another classic statement! *If you don't watch your tongue, girl, you're looking at precisely the man who won't feel a tremor in his soul as he wrenches it from your mouth!*

But again he let it pass without a crack in his mask-like visage.

"It is my very deep hope, Miss Yang, that we can continue to work together. In fact, I am hoping for a very, *very* close relationship."

"I comprehend that fully, Colonel Chou—"

"And, still, you feel you must have time *to consider.*"

She bowed. "It is not every day that a girl is asked to change her—her status, Colonel Chou. I trust you will appreciate the momentousness of the decision you ask me to consider."

"I well appreciate it, Miss Yang. But I wish you to appreciate the sense of urgency which forces me to be so pressing. Three days, Miss Yang. That is all the time which remains." He took her hand, shook it as if it were a fish, then smiled. "All the time which remains."

Three days.

Through the window she watched the man's back as it receded into the darkness between her building and that toward which he was headed. Beyond, the moonlight showed the high fence and a moonbeam, or starlight perhaps, illuminated a guard with what seemed to be a very effective machine gun.

Three days.

Someone will be coming.

She looked up at the stars. *Perhaps, Father. Perhaps you are right. But does the someone you spoke of know that if he comes four days from now, he will have come all this way for nothing?*

She stepped back from the window as if in shock, looking at her own reflection upon the glass. *For nothing.* What did she mean by that? That she'd be gone—gone with Colonel Chou to this place called Chirkee or

83

Chickee or whatever? Is that what she'd meant? Or did she instead mean that she had no intention of accompanying that dreaded little man anywhere at any time? What did she mean?

"Father—what did I mean?" she asked quietly.

But her father did not answer.

CHAPTER 9

The break of dawn found Eagle's legs still taking long graceful strides, moving him steadily across the landscape which before his travels were over would vary from rocky hillocks to thin forests and from lush green vegetation to burnt-out fields of dust. He ran as if he were not a man or even an animal, but as if he were some highly efficient machine. Leg whipped past leg and thrust forward with the minimum of effort and minimum pressure to move the machine ahead. His breathing was deep and easy, but steady. His mind and body were as one.

At regular intervals, usually after two or three hours of steady pacing, he had stopped during the night for rest periods of fifteen minutes. Even the most efficient of machines cannot run steadily forever and after each rest period, the machine with the code name Expeditor was rejuvenated. Twice during the night he had taken a small pill from one of the pockets in his suit. It was a combination food and water pill, designed to give the body what it needed for sustenance. A scientific version of the *pemmican* of his adoptive people, it was no gourmet's delight, but it served its purpose. Eagle had several of the little pills with him, more than enough for the length of time this mission was supposed to take.

As now he chose the crest of a hill to take another rest period, he let his mind actively consider something other than the task of running.

He thought about time.

By late afternoon he would be at the Hsi tributary. If he chose to continue overland to the Pei, he would reach that by early morning. Depending upon his mode of transport upward along that river, it would take him anywhere from eight to twenty-four hours to reach target. If the longer time, he would then have been within China for what was beginning his fourth day. All of which left him another three full days to return south and rendezvous with the submarine which would be waiting offshore. Merlin had argued for allowing four days for the return trip. "You're forgetting, John, you'll have the girl with you." Eagle admitted she might not have the stamina necessary for long-distance running, "but that probably won't be needed. We've got the river flowing with us. The Pei and its tributaries flow conveniently into Macao." It was to be somewhat west of that Portuguese territory that the sub would be waiting.

"All right," Merlin had conceded. "You'll have your sub offshore seven days after you board the train to Hong Kong. But if your signal isn't heard then . . ." He didn't have to finish. The waters off the coast of Red China were no place to be playing games in. In any case, Eagle would cross that bridge when he came

85

to it. His muscles were already growing impatient to begin functioning again.

It went according to schedule. At four thirty that afternoon he was stroking the waters of the Hsi, his body enjoying the reprieve from running vertically upright and the demands now placed upon it in his horizontally stretched-out position. He purposely used his arms more than was necessary, more than was correct form, allowing his legs merely to stretch and giving his shoulders and back a chance to come to some bodily equilibrium with the lower muscles. Because the river was not wide enough for this purpose, he swam straight upstream against the current for about fifteen minutes, counting this as a rest break he would not have to take later. When he did emerge silently from the water, he took another of his food pills. Then his legs swung into action.

Through the night they swung, mile after mile passing behind them, the Chinese stars over his head blinking with curiosity down at this lone stranger whom they could not be certain was there, so well did the movement below blend into the dull moonscape. And it was now that Eagle began to feel the euphoria of being one with the universe, that strange feeling that the Chinese sages of old—and the sages of his own people as well—had understood so deeply. It was a blending, a melding that modern philosophers liked to talk about, but it was a state of being which one did not achieve by talking, not even in the fullest of book-lined studies nor in the sparsest of Zen monasteries. The old mystics understood the cosmos as motion, and it was by motion—mindless motion—that the individual being became part of the One which is the All. Far from being a dangerous state of mind, it was one which was extremely helpful—for somehow the mind in this condition could see and hear and feel things which normal

86

senses or even those of a keen-sensed animal could not register. Thus was Eagle able now to sense the presence of other beings—people and animals—which were far out of his abnormally excellent sensory range, and thus was he able to avoid completely unwanted contact.

So the stars blinked, then they laughed. And Eagle, as part of them and the larger All, laughed with them.

He reached the Pei about two hours before dawn, in time to hitch a ride on the rear end of a small flat barge-type vessel which was moving northward at a moderately good rate. There was a small, one-room cabin fashioned of rusty corrugated steel perched upon the stern of the boat, and as Eagle pulled himself quietly on board, he saw that there was but one old man inside, busy at the wheel. Smiling, the invisible man silently lifted himself up onto the flat roof. He stretched out his long limbs and slept.

He had counted on anywhere between eight and twenty-four hours to make the upriver part of the journey. In actual fact he slipped into the water and began striking out for shore fourteen hours after he'd climbed aboard the little barge. That vessel had gone only as far as the riverside town of Ying-te, however, and there Eagle had hitched another ride, this time at the rear of a river patrol boat. He considered the mode of transport fortunate, in that this was undoubtedly the fastest vessel on the river and, for later reference, he wanted to study its operations. He had just enough time to do so when, unfortunately, the boat swung around and began heading south. Again Eagle transferred, this time to another flatboat, larger and just a bit faster than the first. Now he began to get impatient, his muscles aching to get into the water, then onto the land where again they could flex and take the landscape at their own pace. But he stayed with the craft, knowing that, while perhaps he could make better speed straight-line-running, there was an additional benefit of his taking the river all the way. Knowledge, that was the benefit. Knowledge of the specifics of the river which probably would be his escape route, knowledge of the official patrol boats which he would have to avoid. For although the way downriver might be faster, it might be heavier going.

No one, after all, was expecting an intruder on this leg of the mission. But on the way down, after the fireworks . . .

And he fully expected there would be fireworks.

The strip-watch on his wrist told him that the time was ten-thirty. It had taken him two hours after leaving the Pei to locate the compound and the next forty-five minutes he'd spent moving around it in the darkness, slipping between the spotlights which at regular intervals bathed the ground with their brilliance. Points of interests were the four machine-gun towers, all manned, the positions of other guard units and the buildings which were being guarded. Even before the tour, however, he was well aware of his four basic problems:

One, to get inside.

Two, to locate the girl.

Three, to destroy everything in sight.

Four, to get himself and the girl out safely.

Reverse three and four? Possible—if he had been armed with his usual equipment. His alloy bow could send from a safe distance any number of explosive-headed arrows to level the place. His pitching arm wasn't quite good enough. In any case, first things first.

One, to get inside.

The high cross-hatched wire fence was a barrier in two ways. Outward-slanting barbed wire topped it, and it was electrified. Best way in, then, was through the front gate. But the gate was closed, two guards standing diligently sleepy on the other side. He considered one of the several vials in his pocket. No, he needed them for more important work. And they were noisy. He wanted to keep the noise level down until he found the girl.

In a silent crouch he approached the gate. Unlike the rest of the fence, the crossings of the wire were less close together. If he could reach in and disconnect lock . . .

No, that would trip the alarm. The extra wires were obvious in the way they snaked along the ground to the small guard stand resembling on outhouse. Any living thing touching that fence would send a howling scream into the night in stereo. Anything—

Or anyone.

Eagle smiled. He knew now how he was going to get that gate open. The only problem was . . .

His hand went automatically to the underarm pocket of his suit. The Tokarev was there, awaiting its call to be of service. Damn it. Again he wished he had his own equipment. His usual pistol—the deadly weapon which fired sharp steel spines with accuracy of up to fifty yards—was powered by CO_2 and its noise level was no more than a faint whisper. If he had that Luger-like weapon in his fist right now, all he would have to do is send one of its needles carefully into that guard who was closest to the fence. When he fell forward . . .

But he didn't have the CO_2 pistol. He'd have to handle things without it. It took him only another six seconds to assess the importance of the gap between the ground and the base bar of the fence.

It was about eight inches, and those eight inches held the solution to the entire problem.

Quietly Eagle moved in a slow crawl to the base of the gate. If one of the guards had looked at that particular spot on the lighted ground through the cross-hatchings, he would have seen nothing more than what appeared to be a slight rearrangement of the shadows cast by the uneven ruts in the earth.

But neither man looked. They were looking at each other at the moment. One of them, the one nearest Eagle and with his back turned to the gate, was talking. From the expression on the other's face, it appeared to be a story of the smutty kind. Eagle nodded. What the hell else was there for two men who were on guard duty out here to do?

Well, for one thing, they could die. One of them, anyway, was about to do just that.

With slow movements Eagle's gloved hand unzippered the pocket over his left bicep, then went inside it to wrap around one of the three ammunition clips for the Russian pistol. Placing it under his prone body for the moment, he reclosed the pocket, then reached out for a small rock which lay just about where he wanted it under the fence. Just about wasn't good enough, however. This had to be fairly precise. Wrapping his invisible hand about the piece of stone he moved to the right, checking its position with the electric gate latch. He smiled to himself, then left the rock to take out the ammunition clip from under his chest.

The clip made a sharp *clack* as Eagle placed it heavily against the rock. If he positioned the thing right, the lights would clearly show the metal object and—

The nearest guard turned, looking downward—straight into Eagle's eyes, or rather the gloved hand which hid them. The eyes of the Chinese narrowed, a puzzled look coming over his face. The other guard said something, but the closer one waved his hand for silence. Then, resting his rifle against the guard shack, he stepped forward.

He squatted down, peering at the metal clip.

His right hand moved toward it, then stopped inches from the thing. His expression was even more puzzled now. He said something to the second guard. Then his fingers went the rest of the distance.

And froze—as did the features of his face. They, however, were frozen in horror.

Something had his hand! Something he couldn't see held his hand like a vise! And for just a split second, he was looking into another pair of eyes—laughing, deadly eyes!

Eagle pulled on the hand. The scream began an instant before the man crashed into the fence. It ended with the sizzling, cloth- and flesh-burning contact which brought with it the whine of a siren. Eagle could feel the tremors of electricity run the length of his protective suit as he took the ammunition clip from the hands of the Chinese and rose to the latch.

The other guard was screaming now—over the telephone in the guard shack. He had left his weapon unattended. Good, that was a sign that he viewed his friend's death as nothing more than a clumsy accident. When Eagle pushed on the gate to open it to a degree just enough to slip through, the guard's head jerked toward the opening. The Chinese frowned. Again good. The opening obviously was a result of the accident.

Several pairs of boots were now running toward the gate. Eagle avoided the wearers of the boots. He had completed his first task. Now for the others.

The colonel and the girl had been in one of the hatcheries when the siren wailed. He had requested that she prepare a complete inventory of the equipment which was to be shipped northward the following day. "It is not that I do not trust those who are to perform the jobs of crating and transporting, but a detailed list will assist in keeping honest people honest."

"Northward?" she had asked. "Is that the new location of the project?"

He had shaken his head. "The equipment goes north. At our new location, we have enough of what we shall need. I may tell you that our new location will not be in China, Miss Yang. Does the idea of foreign travel intrigue you?"

"I have not thought much on leaving China," she said. It was of course a lie. She had thought of little else in the past three days and nights.

"And of our previous discussion—have you thought on that?"

"Yes. I have not, however, completely decided how best I can serve my country."

"The time grows late, Miss Yang."

"I fully understand that, Colonel."

He pursed his lips. "I wonder if you do. In any event, I must press for a decision. Now."

"Now?"

The siren stopped his affirmative nod in mid-nod. "Remain here!" he commanded her, already running from the room. But she acted as if she didn't hear him, walking as if in a daze from the place and to the outside. The siren—and men shouting—did this mean . . .

They were all running toward the main gate. Why? What had happened? *Someone will come. . . .*

How long she stood there, or whether she was standing or walking when the voice spoke to her, she didn't know.

"What is reality, Miss Yang?"

"Reality is—" She stopped, the jarring thought crashing through her mind that she was hearing English and that she had answered in the same language. But—

No one was there.

No one!

But there had to be, because—

Something had taken her hand, opened it and placed something in her palm.

A piece of paper. A letter, very short and to the point. And at its end—

Her father's mark.

"Walk to a place where we can be alone. I will show myself to you then. Can you understand what I'm saying?"

She nodded dumbly, then turned to the nearest building. Smaller than those around it, it looked like a toolshed. Yes, that's what it was. One long room with a door and one window at the opposite wall, it was the place where the maintenance crew kept tools and spare equipment.

"No lights," the voice—a strong male voice—told her as she watched the door close seemingly by itself. Then she saw the man who owned the voice. His left hand was doing something behind his left knee. "The suit—it has special properties," he told her. "I have one for you. Undress and put it on—quickly."

She looked at the flat bundle which he seemed somehow to detach from behind his back. "Undress

"Your clothes—take them off. Quickly. I'll help you into this."

"I have never before—"

"Miss Yang, I'm not interested in what you've done or not done before. Furthermore, I'm not interested in your body. Simply do as I say. I've come a long way to reach you, and I have very little patience with shyness."

She looked from the bundle to the man's eyes. Otherwise his head was covered. She wanted to see—

The man obviously understood. He detached the mask and pulled back the hood. His face was rough like a young mountain, needing a shave. His blue eyes were clear—and somehow fierce—but fierceness was tempered by a gentleness. She wondered at that moment whether or not this man even suspected the gentleness he contained within him. She suspected that he did not—especially when he reached a gloved hand toward her and ripped off her laboratory coat.

"I said quickly!" Then his voice softened. "Please, Miss Yang."

She nodded and bent to the task, her mind acutely aware of the way his eyes moved over her body as the last of her underclothing fell to the floor. And she suspected—as well as hoped somewhere within her—that he had not been telling the truth when he had said that he was not interested in her body. It was not at all the proper thing even to think, but she recognized the thought—or feeling, whichever it was—and was not as ashamed in that thought or feeling as she recognized she ought to be.

And then his hands took her once more, grasping her thighs firmly as he placed—gently, yes!—her feet into the legs of the strangely thin garment, holding her shoulders as he pulled the material up and around them, guiding her hands and arms to where they should be, his shoulder brushing against her breasts ever so slightly, then his fingers manipulating the finely constructed zippers, fingers which felt thick and strong through the material of the gloves, but which touched her with a gentleness she never had associated with the touch of a man.

Gentle. Yes, this tall firm man was gentle.

Such was her thought when the door to the toolshed opened.

Of the four men who stood half stunned in the doorway, two of them wore uniforms and carried rifles. One of the rifles was pointed directly at her.

It fired.

CHAPTER 10

Eagle cursed to himself. He had been singularly stupid! Of course—one of the first places they would come to would be the place where the tools were kept. The damned gate system would have to be repaired, and to where else would the repairmen be dispatched—where else but ye olde toolshed? To add to his problems, two of the men weren't repairmen—and one of them—

Eagle's body went into action. With the palm of his left hand he shoved the girl from the point-blank position she held with respect to the raising rifle. Even so, the rifleman's reflexes were quick and his mind made up as to who was to receive his first shot. Simultaneous to the roar of the weapon, Eagle heard the girl's gasp from behind him. From the corner of his eye he saw her slam against the wall clutching her arm, as with a vengeance he launched himself at the four men.

They were standing in a tight group—too tight for their own good, they learned, as Eagle collided with the first rifleman. It was much like a bowling-pin action, the first two men remaining standing, although staggering backward, and the two who were completely outside the shack landing on their butts in the dirt. With his left hand, Eagle gripped the most forward rifle midway down the barrel and tore it from the Chinese soldier's grasp. Then, allowing the momentum from the powerful jerk to carry around circularly over his head, Eagle sent the stock of the weapon crunching into the side of the second standing man's skull. The soldier whose rifle had been used as a bludgeon stared at his fallen companion—one of the civilians—for but a moment. That's all the time he had before Eagle's heel drove into his solar plexus with instantaneous death.

The other two were up now and charging. One of them was the other rifleman who was sighting up his target at close range. The other, the second civilian, was a squat, heavy-set man with the face of a rhinoceros and thick arms to match. That was the one Eagle kept in his primary focus as with a quick step forward he pull-pushed the unsteady rifle, steel butt-plate first, painfully into the teeth of its carrier. As the soldier began to choke on his own blood, Eagle stepped backward to meet the rhino.

The squat man was in no rush. His advance was a series of side-gliding foot motions that spoke volumes about his training as did the raised hands which were held in the "bent chicken wrist" fashion of the *pau-kau* expert. The tight grin on his face told his opponent that he expected the business to be finished summarily.

It was—because, even though the rhino was in no hurry, Eagle could already hear the sounds of running feet getting louder. Eagle therefore launched a flying kick, shoving off with his right and sending his left like an arrow at the thick-set head. The rhino, moving quickly to the left and outside of the oncoming attack, swept his left forearm around in what was a perfectly executed slack block—or what would have been, if Eagle's leg still was there. It wasn't.

The feint having achieved Eagle's purpose, he drove his left foot to the floor like a sledgehammer and in a lightning-like move, positioned himself directly behind the squat man. Even before the Chinese had a chance to turn, Eagle's hands were somehow on him and under him. There was a sudden twist and a surge of almost superhuman power. The Chinese screamed as his feet left the floor and he saw the glass of the window rushing toward him like a jet. With a shattering blast of splintering glass and window frame, the rhino left the building. He did not rise from the crumpled position at which he came to rest.

Eagle swiftly took the girl by the shoulders. "You're all right?"

"I've been shot!"

"Yes." He saw where she held her hand over the sleeve of the suit. He took her hand from the spot. There was no mark there. "One of the advantages of your new clothes. You're lucky he didn't get you *here*." His hand lightly touched her bare breast as he completed fastening the front of the suit. "The mask and hood—put them on while I—"

He bent down, his fingers moving around to behind her left knee. In an instant he stepped from her. Yes, except for her face and hair where she was not yet covered by the plastic material, she blended nicely into the dark background. The second chameleon unit was working perfectly.

He switched his own unit on, his invisible hands completing the covering of her head. Then, from a pocket at his right shin, he took out two identical objects. "One more thing to fit around your head," he said. When both pair of thin celluloid "glasses" were in place in front of their eyes, they could see each other's forms, even with the chameleon units working at maximum efficiency. Development of the glasses had been ordered by Merlin on a rush basis, once Eagle had explained a practical problem with two invisible people traveling together. "My God, John, you're right," the

97

old man had said. "You could be wandering around for days just looking for her!"

The sounds of feet and voices were all around them now. "Ready?" Eagle asked in a whisper. When she nodded her head yes, he motioned toward the window. "We'll go that way. Me first, then you. Very, very slowly and quietly. Keep close to walls—and away from light." Again she nodded as Eagle took her hand and led the way. He had one foot over the sill as the first of the soldiers stormed through the open door. Suddenly the hand by which Eagle had held the girl was empty. She was a blurred motion, her right leg executing a perfect crescent kick to the soldier's left temple. He dropped, his rifle clattering beneath him.

"Well done," Eagle whispered appreciatively as she rejoined him.

"Everybody has to have—what would you say—a hobby," she answered.

"A good choice, but not a good choice of time. Come on!"

He dropped to the ground lightly on the balls of his feet, then turned and assisted the girl. All around them now were nervous eyes and guns. As they began to weave their way through them, Eagle heard someone shouting out fierce orders from the far side of the shack where the door was.

"Colonel Chou," the girl whispered to him. "He is in charge here." She began to move in the direction of the voice.

"No." Eagle's grip on her wrist tightened. He pulled her into the shadows between two buildings. "First, where are the Devils?"

"Devils?"

"The insects—the destroyer insects."

"They are not here. Not the ones you seek. The ones you seek have been moved."

98

Eagle repeated her final word. "Where—to where have they been moved?"

"Colonel Chou said they had been taken from China."

Eagle nodded. It squared with what Merlin had figured. The only thing was they had moved the damned bugs too soon. He reached into his pocket.

"What are they?" she asked, looking at the dozen or so colored vials in his gloved hand.

He told her, his hands busily turning the white caps on all of the green vials. This time he clicked off several turns to the left rather than to the right. Instead of exploding upon contact now the grenades would go off at a predetermined time. Two minutes was the setting. He told her that too as he gave her five of the vials.

"Those five buildings. Just make sure a vial is inside each. When you've placed them, go to the main gate. I'll meet you there."

"But—those are just dormitories. Sleeping places."

"You heard me. My orders are to destroy this place totally."

She paused for a moment. "And kill everyone within?"

"Not everyone. Not you."

"But—there are others, workers and technicians who had no idea of what work was being done here."

He nodded. "I doubt that they—or anybody—will be inside any of the buildings when they go up, but all right. We'll give the noncombatants a chance. Here." He took the vials from her and changed the cap settings. "That will give them an extra thirty seconds. When it becomes apparent that all the buildings are blowing up, those who are inside the dormitories, if they are smart, will leave."

"And those who are not smart?"

His voice was hard. "They'll be casualties of war,

Miss Yang. Perhaps you haven't absorbed the fact that that's what we're engaged in—a war. Speaking of which, we've just used up about twenty seconds of combat time. Move—then to the gate. Understand?"

The girl scampered from the place, Eagle moving swiftly in the opposite direction. And now as he ran between clusters of confused Chinese, the earlier work of reconnoitering the complex paid its dividends. He ran in pattern, in an efficient, diagonally changing pattern, which brought him to the target areas in the least number of steps possible. At each building, one of the green vials was left behind. Where a door or window was open, the unseen running man did not have to break his stride. Where such was not the case, the bringer of glass-enclosed death had to make an opening. In two cases it took no more than the silent turning of a knob. In one, because the door was not conveniently placed, Eagle smashed a window pane with his fist, then opened his fingers to allow gravity to carry the green vial to the floor within.

His last building target—the seventh—was the toolshed. As the vial was gently placed just within the door, he saw a thin uniformed Chinese screaming in a strident voice at other soldiers. It was the voice which the girl had identified as belonging to Colonel Chou. Eagle was about to move toward the man, to kill him with his hands, then his eyes fell to his strip-watch. No. There wasn't time to play games. Because there were two more targets he wanted to make sure were completely out of commission.

Bidding Colonel Chou a silent farewell, he left the man to die in his own way.

He had noticed them during the time he had circled the fence earlier. Two motor vehicles, one of them a heavy-duty truck which looked to be of World War II vintage, and the other a battered staff car, probably belonging to the colonel. They appeared to be the only

100

effective escape vehicles on the grounds, and Eagle wanted them inoperative.

Well, not quite inoperative. He hadn't time to fool around with anything under the hood. Reaching them now, he opened the driver's side door of the truck and placed one of his vials—purple this time—under the top part of the accelerator pedal. The cap was twisted to the right. Impact setting. The staff car got the same gift. Eagle grinned tightly inside his mask. Anyone planning a quick trip would be traveling a hell of a lot farther than he planned. And in a good many more directions as well.

Another glance at the strip-watch. Twenty seconds to go. He moved out toward the gate.

She was waiting for him as he had ordered her. Good. The last thing he'd wanted to have to do was to hunt for her in and around the holocaust which was to come. But for the moment, he left her where she was. Her face was turned toward him and he knew that she could see him. Fine. She was now to get a picture of what this war was all about. It would be, he hoped, a picture that would stand her—and him—in good stead in the event that the going got really heavy during the next couple of days. In the meantime, he needed an effective weapon, and it took no thought at all on his part to make his choice.

In quick long strides he was at the base of the nearest wood-beamed tower which held the searchlight and the machine gun. His hands and feet found their holdings rapidly and within instants he was at the top. There was a lone soldier tending the place, leaning over the inside rail and peering downward to try to determine the cause of all the commotion below.

With one hand to the seat of the soldier's pants, Eagle lifted him up and over the railing. The man's scream ended abruptly as his back slapped to the

101

earth. Eagle did not bother to watch the landing. He was too busy swinging the heavy gun—a real antique by the look of it—around so that it faced the interior of the compound.

Quickly now his eyes scanned the other three towers. Only one of them was occupied—the nearest. Excellent luck. His main targets were below; he didn't want to waste ammunition cleaning out the crows' nests. Nonetheless, he would earmark the first burst for his fellow gunman. The muzzle of the machine gun aligned itself accordingly as Eagle again checked his strip-watch.

Nine seconds. Eight . . . seven . . .

From the corner of his eye now he saw something move toward him. A flash of gray, crossing from the area of the gate to the tower. *The girl!*

Five . . . four . . .

Good God! *"No!"* he roared. "Stay there—*and hit the ground!"*

Two . . . one . . .

The ground before him seemed to open up as if hell itself had finally pushed through to the surface. As metal and wood and flesh and bone were driven up into the night under some half dozen bright orange suns, Eagle had no chance to see whether the girl had obeyed his command. His finger was slowly squeezing the machine gun trigger.

First target—the gunner in the other tower. Eagle's first burst caught him high in the chest, driving the man halfway up to his feet and slamming him into the railing to his back. Neither the railing nor the upright beam which held it in place were strong enough to withstand the impact and, with the sharp splintering and dull crushing sounds which came from a mixture of good and rotted wood, the dead man cleared the tower and fell onto the barbed wire of the fence below. The fence sparked into life, hissing and crackling around the body of the corpse which dangled from its upper reaches. Eagle nodded appreciatively. The maintenance boys had been fast workers. Probably because they didn't have any labor unions around here, he decided.

As he swung the big weapon down into the compound, something whizzed by his ear like an enraged hornet. Instinctively, he looked down toward his left. The lone rifleman was taking a second aim. Screw him, Eagle mumbled through his teeth, and he was about to dismiss him from his thoughts when what looked like a gray ghost leaped toward the rifleman and with a hand-blade chop to the bridge of his nose sent the soldier crumbling to earth.

An excellent choice for—how you call it?—a hobby, yes.

But enough merriment.

The big gun opened up. Short burst followed short burst. Men dropped screaming, either from the holes the machine gun was putting in their chests and stomachs or from pain caused by flaming clothing and skin or from a sudden fiery loss of limb. The ammunition for the weapon was ample, Eagle decided, so he spent it freely, attempting to single out those who wore warrior green. But that was not all that easy, as the condition of what may have been technician's white had changed radically.

Again he looked at the strip-watch. If the girl had done as he'd told her, those remaining five buildings—

New orange suns were born in the compound beneath him, taking two of the towers down under the onslaught of shock wave and free-flying shrapnel. New screams were added to old, and from them Eagle knew that he had been wrong about where the technicians would choose to remain. The fact that those who had ventured out into the rubble-strewn clearing had met death from his still screaming weapon probably played its part in convincing many of them that it was safer inside the doubtful protection of corrugated steel. Either way, he had killed them.

"And the people you have killed," White Deer had said. *"Have they deserved death from your hands?"*

"Yes, my mother."

"And who decides whom you will kill? Yourself?"

"No. Another. Another for whom I work."

"He is a good man, this man for whom you kill? He does not order the deaths of innocent people?"

"He does not order—and I do not execute—the deaths of innocent people."

Except, he said to himself, under conditions of war. An undeclared war, perhaps, a war which to the Apache—*because* it was undeclared—would not be an honorable war. But the Apache nation had come to an end in large part because they had behaved with honor to men who did not behave the same way. Meeting lies with truth, meeting duplicity with honesty, the Apache fell. No, that was not true, and he knew it. He knew that if he had ever said these words to the man he had loved so much, his old grandfather Ho-kwa-sikna, the old man's eyes would flood with a combined anger and sorrow. *No, my son. The Apache has fallen only by the white man's standards. If the Apache's spirit has been honest with itself and true to its ways, it can stand proudly without regard to circumstances outside itself.*

And now Eagle grimaced. His grandfather was right, but he also was wrong. The false standards were not only those of the white man. They were yellow men's standards too—and those of black men. They were the standards of these times. And it was the times which his grandfather—and his mother, too—could not fully understand. As for himself—

But he broke off his line of thinking. A group of three had come into the clearing below.

The big machine gun spoke out its chattering death.

The snapping and crackling of flames were all the sounds they heard as the two of them walked through the embers and ashes and the dead husks of what had been buildings and machines and men. Someone, Eagle saw, had attempted to start the staff car. It was totally demolished. There was no evidence of the man who had stepped on the accelerator, unless that one lone boot, some yards away from the spot . . .

"They all are dead," the girl said. It was not quite a true statement. Eagle had seen at least three men who were still alive. If they had been near death, he would have used the Tokarev to put them out of their misery, but none of the three was hurt badly. Still he did not contradict the girl. To do so might push her mind into new channels, some mission of mercy.

She repeated the statement. When still he didn't reply, she stopped and looked at him. "Why do we linger here? Do we not have to escape before someone else comes? Or is it that you wish to kill more?"

He turned on her fiercely, but said nothing until the brightness of his eyes quieted. "I'm looking for Colonel Chou. I want to make sure he is dead."

She shook her head. "Most probably, he is here with the others. Not many of them are such as to be able to recognize them."

"Perhaps. Tell me, did he have some kind of special escape route, some kind of special hiding place?"

She did not know, which Eagle expected would be the case. For the old-line Chinese, such a route or hiding place would be standard operating procedure. As to the *new* Chinese, he didn't know, but putting on a new suit of clothes did not make a new man, and putting on a new set of political truths did not change the basic instinct of survival.

"His main headquarters. Which building?"

It was a pile of rubble and twisted sheet metal. Moving around it, Eagle's every sense remained alert for even the smallest evidence of movement. None registered.

"All right, Miss Yang, we leave for the river. Take a last look around. And prepare yourself."

"Prepare?"

He nodded. "The worst is yet to come."

As they moved from the spot, another head nodded, but only slightly. If Colonel Chou had his way, that phrase in English would be its speaker's epitaph.

CHAPTER 11

The worst is yet to come.

Colonel Chou waited for fifteen full minutes before he moved from his hiding place. The American— American, yes; the colonel had taken much instruction in the English language as part of his intelligence training, and he knew the differences with which the tongue was pronounced by those peoples who used it—the American had been very clever. He had known there would be a secret hiding place. What he had not known was that the colonel had no way of getting to it, not once his office building was blown up. And the American and the girl—he was sure it was the Yang girl—had stood so very close to where the colonel was hiding.

In the rear of the old truck, hunched under the seat and covered by a smelly tarp—that's where the colonel had taken himself once the going got rough. At one point, one of the enlisted men jumped into the front of the vehicle in an attempt to break out of the compound, but a bullet from the colonel's gun had stopped the attempt even before the man had the door closed.

But now all was quiet. The American and the girl had gone, and it was time for the colonel to count his losses.

As he stepped down from the rear of the truck, Colonel Chou's eyes widened. So much damage . . . so much destruction. . . . One man had done all this. One man had somehow gotten into the compound and—*and done all this!*

He walked through what, seemingly a lifetime ago, had been his command. His walking was unhurried, not only because of the state of his mind, but because of his wounds. The blood had dried upon his right thigh and his right elbow. He had been lucky, very lucky. Unlike all these others, he was alive. The one man among all of them which the American had missed.

Lucky.

But was he? What did he do now? He would have to report this to someone of higher authority, would he not? And when he did that, the higher authority surely would want to know just what it was about these facilities which made them a target for such destruction. To have acted on his own as he had—to have taken all of the responsibility upon his own shoulders as he had . . .

107

But he had been right! They, all of them, would have seen that when single-handedly *he* and he alone had brought the proud Americans to their knees. But instead . . .

No. He still could do it. The arrangements for his departure all had been made. His departure and hers. *Her*. A traitor, just like her father. But, then, Dr. Yang had not been a traitor, had he? No, but he would have been, Colonel Chou was certain of it. Had the good doctor known what the real mission of the project was, the mission Colonel Chou himself had authorized and implemented with no authority other than his own . . .

But he could still do it! His command post at Shao-kuan, twenty miles west of here. The men there were *his* men. They would do as he ordered. Yes, at Shao-kuan. . . .

A sound broke off his attempt at planning. His pistol snapped forward as his eyes tried to detect movement in the spaces of darkness between the flaming embers which surrounded him. There it was again. A voice.

A groan.

It was one of the technicians. Colonel Chou found him lying on his back, a bloodied gash across his forehead, his eyes staring upward toward the barrel of the colonel's pistol. "Colonel . . ."

"Get on your feet if you can. Can you move?"

The man tried, his eyes questioning why the officer did not try to assist him. As the man did make it to a wobbling standing position, the colonel explained why:

"I need a man who can function. I have no need for anyone now who cannot obey my orders. Is anyone else still alive?"

"I—I don't know, Colonel. . . ."

"Very well. I must see for myself. There is a truck on the east side of the compound. Go to it and drive it to the gate. I will meet you there."

As the man stumbled in the direction indicated by the colonel's pistol barrel, the colonel himself walked slowly in the direction of the gate. It was then he heard another sound—one which was not caused by his own or the other survivor's feet touching the earth.

It was the grating of metal against metal.

His face was grim as he edged around what remained of one leaning wall of what had been one of the technicians' dormitories. He moved silently, but not silently enough. The slight figure leaning over something on the ground stood up as if he had been struck by lightning.

Correction: as if *she* had been struck by lightning.

"Colonel Chou!" She bowed slightly, then stepped away so that he could see the mechanism on the ground.

It was a bicycle. "I have made some repairs, sir. The tires were intact and the wheels, although bent, should be workable—"

The colonel smiled nastily. "I have no need of your toy, young woman!"

As if punctuating the sentence came the sound which rendered it erroneous. The sky was lighted up anew by the lone explosion.

Hobbling to a point where he could see the source of the flames, Colonel Chou cursed at the sky—even though before his eyes returned the evidence he knew within him what the explosion was all about. He had seen earlier the gutted staff car. Now . . .

He returned to the woman. "It appears I must retract my statement, I am afraid."

She was sitting astride the two-wheeled device. She nodded and stepped from it, extending the handle bars to him. "I understand, Colonel. In any case, I do not live far from here. In the village, in fact. I can walk the short distance easily."

"No, I don't believe you can."

She looked down at the blood which matted the front of her shoulder. "My wound? It is not serious, Colonel."

"I was not talking about your wound." His voice was like steel. "I was referring to the fact that I simply cannot have you speaking to anyone about what has happened here tonight."

"Colonel?" She let go of the bike, her eyes growing very wide.

There was stark fear upon her face as her commanding officer lifted his pistol and fired two bullets through her forehead.

He rode the wobbling unsteady two-wheeler into the village of Shih-hsing. He had no knowledge of how much time the trip had taken, and he had met no one on the way. Purposely he had caused the villagers to hear stories that the scientific facilities were dealing with deadly germs and that they should never get close to the installation. Even now he almost could grin at the effectiveness of the propaganda. With all the fireworks, no one had come to investigate or help. No one. Now that he considered it, that fact made him angry. There was one man who definitely should have come— and fast.

His anger remained in the midst of what was almost total exhaustion as he rapped upon the door of a small house near the village outskirts. After a time, the door opened speculatively, then widened.

"*Colonel Chou, sir!*" the man in the nightshirt exclaimed. "What has happened?"

"In that you didn't find it convenient to come and see for yourself, Captain, I shall explain that only to the proper authorities," the colonel said as he stumbled into the room. "Hurry and dress yourself. You must drive me to Shao-kuan at once."

"But, sir—I have no car!"

Colonel Chou fell into the lone chair in the room. "Captain, do not argue with me. You have your orders. Get dressed, then get a car. Commandeer one. And, Captain—no one is to know of my presence here. Is that understood?"

"Yes sir, but—"

"You have your orders, Captain," the colonel said. Then, his body issuing its own command through its own needs, his head leaned forward onto the table top and his eyes closed in the sleep of exhaustion.

When he awoke he was in the front seat of some kind of small vehicle, the interior of which had a putrid smell that fouled his nostrils and burned his watering eyes. "Captain, what in the People's name—"

"Sorry, sir, the only vehicle available for commandeering was this one. I was hoping you'd remain asleep. It's a farmer's truck, sir, a chicken farmer's—"

"Chicken shit!"

"Er, yes sir."

Mercifully, sleep again claimed Colonel Chou.

He awoke abruptly as he became aware that his body was being handled.

"It's all right, Colonel," someone was saying. "Hurry! Help the Colonel!"

The clock in the office said it was forty minutes past midnight. Colonel Chou had washed himself quickly and sipped of *mo tai,* a potent Chinese rice wine. A change of clothing lay upon the chair behind him, but his main interest was in the large map which dominated one full office wall. His eyes focused along the length of the River Pei as if he were a madman, yet the junior officer who headed the Shao-kuan headquarters under Colonel Chou's command could not but admire his senior's dedication to duty, even though he thought the colonel had at least one of his facts wrong.

"Colonel, if this is the man I think he may be, he's

111

not American. He's Russian. Three days ago, according to this report—"

"Never mind your report—and never mind what nationality he is. I want him. Do you hear me? I want him dead—and the woman, too."

"Yes, sir."

"Now. I want patrol boats spread out here . . . and here . . . and here." He pointed to the places on the map with a sharp letter opener he had taken from the junior officer's desk. "Surely, they will take the river south as the fastest way. They have no food, and I do not think they have any way of getting any assistance until they leave the country."

"You are certain that is what they will do—leave the country?"

Colonel Chou's eyes spat fire. "If he is American or Russian or whatever he is, do you think he intends to stay within our borders?" He calmed himself down. "I beg your pardon, there is no need for me to shout at you. Between the two of us, what I have uncovered is a gross plot against our Republic. The Yang woman, and, I suspect, her father, whom I have liquidated, was involved in a monstrous plot to develop an insect which would destroy our agricultural economy. They must be stopped, I cannot stress enough the importance of our doing that. You, sir, must direct that work. I myself must proceed downriver at once."

"To intercept them, sir?"

The colonel shook his head. "No. I have made arrangements to squash them at their other location. I cannot tell you where it is, I am sorry to say. But as soon as you have deployed the patrol boats as I have directed, I will be on my way."

"But, Colonel—"

"Give the necessary orders!"

"Yes, sir."

Within minutes, the orders were given. Smiling to

himself, Colonel Chou drained his third cup of *mo tai*. Whoever the man was, he and the girl would be dead within hours. The man was an efficient destroyer, yes, but he had made the error of mentioning the fact they were going downriver. That meant the Pei. It could only mean the Pei.

But there was one other matter.

"The captain who brought me here," he said to the officer in charge. "He is to be arrested as a traitor to the people."

"For what reason, sir?"

"I shall fill out the necessary forms. You have ordered a boat for me?"

"Yes, sir, but—"

"But what? When will it be ready?"

"In perhaps fifteen minutes, sir, but—"

The colonel bobbed his head. "I know, I know. I look as if I had just attended all the major battles of the People's Revolution. I shall now change into more suitable clothing. I assume that you have civilian clothing here which will fit my person?"

"Yes, sir, but—"

"You will bring them here at once." When the officer hesitated, the colonel repeated the command. The officer bowed briskly and left the room.

Like sheep, Colonel Chou thought as he stepped to the officer's desk and poured himself another *mo tai*. This would have to be his last. As invigorating and sustaining as the liquid was, he could not afford to have his mental reflexes dulled even a tiny bit. Not now, not when everything had to work like clockwork.

He looked at the clock. Twelve-fifty. And now he smiled at the map. They didn't have a chance. Sheep going to the slaughter. Sheep. Everybody was a sheep.

No, not everybody. But the true revolutionary spirit of Mao had gone from the land, gone from the hearts

113

of the people. Only a few individuals retained it. But when his own exploits were known, when his mission against the United States was accomplished, then once again the fire of the true Chinese character would come to the fore. How could it not, when one of their number—a lone Chinese colonel—had brought to its knees what considered itself the most powerful nation since the beginning of time.

But, in the meantime, there might be one or two difficulties to overcome. He smiled, knowing that he was equal to the task.

A woman brought him the change of clothing he had asked for. Quickly he made the transfer, pausing only to cleanse his wounds. Once on the patrol boat, he could get more complete care. All service boats carried some first-aid equipment, and his wounds were of a superficial nature, luckily.

Yes, luckily. For even though his facilities had been totally destroyed, the destroyer had come a bit too late. The mission could not be halted—could *not* be! Not unless something happened which would not allow him to direct the proceedings at the new location. And that simply wouldn't—

The door opened, the junior officer stepping into the room.

The colonel smiled. "You have obeyed my orders?"

"Yes, sir."

"The captain is under arrest?"

"Yes sir."

"The boat for myself has been ordered?"

"Yes, sir."

"Excellent. Let us proceed then to the harbor." He moved to leave the room, but noticing that the younger man stood where he was, he stopped. "There is something more?"

The man's eyes avoided his. Nodding, the colonel

proceeded to the door and closed it. Then he returned to a spot before the desk behind which the junior man stood.

"Speak," he directed the younger man.

Hesitatingly, the man spoke. "You—did not fill out the forms on the captain, sir."

"Give me the forms. I shall fill them out on the patrol boat and have them sent to you posthaste. May I remind you, that time is of the essence right now."

"I am so reminded, sir."

"Then?"

"There is another, larger matter." The younger man's eyes focused on the top of his desk. "Sir, from what you say the installation at Shih-hsing has been destroyed."

"That is correct."

The eyes lifted, looking straight at the colonel's. "In which case, sir, the destruction must be reported."

"Again, I intend to take care of that. The patrol boat has an operative radio, I assume?"

"Yes, sir, but I think you should make the report now—from here. My commanding officers—"

"*I* am your commanding officer!"

"Yes, sir. One of them."

"*One* of . . ."

"Yes, sir."

Colonel Chou sighed, turning his back for the moment toward the younger man. "I see. . . ."

He *did* see. He should have seen, should have known, long before this. Intelligence work being what it was, intelligence people being what they were . . . of course. He himself, when he was a captain, had served two masters, neither of whom knew of the other. A difficult wire-balancing act, but he had managed it. He had no doubt that this young man had managed it as well, and quite well.

Until now.

"I see," he said. "Very well, what are a few moments more?"

The younger man brightened. The difficult time had passed. He came around the side of the desk, his hand extended. "Colonel, I want you to know that I—"

The smile faded as his open mouth betrayed the sudden terror which commanded his face. There was only an instant when the beginnings of a startled cry rattled upward through his throat.

Just before the very sharp letter opener was plunged into that very throat.

There was a washroom off the office. The young man was dragged there, then the colonel locked the door with the key which was conveniently in its place. He pocketed the key, then entered the outer office. The enlisted man seated behind the desk there snapped to attention.

Colonel Chou smiled. "I believe arrangements have been made to take me to the harbor," he said genially.

The enlisted man rushed to open the outer door for this high-ranking personage.

CHAPTER 12

Eagle was content to let the small canvas-roofed sampan ride the downstream current, but he was careful to keep his eyes alertly alternating from both shorelines to any vessel which came into view regardless of how innocuous. He doubted that the Chinese who owned the boat which they had stolen somewhat northwest of Shih-hsing would discover the theft for several hours. Even then the man might suspect that the vessel had merely come loose from the place it was tied up. But it paid to be ready. Especially since he had not uncovered the corpse of Colonel Chou back at the compound. By all odds, the girl was right when she said he was probably strewn about the place in pieces, but a man in Eagle's work never took his eyes off the gaming table until the final card was turned.

Eagle's work. Expeditor. For all of the girl's intense study of the English language it was a word she'd not learned. She had asked him about himself once she had the chance—which wasn't until they had pushed out into the Pei in the sampan. Prior to that her breath had been busy attempting to keep up with Eagle's striding pace. It was as she flopped clumsily into the bottom of the small boat that she complained in an exhausted rush of breath. "I say this for America—she trains her spies well in physical fitness."

"I'm not a spy," he told her. When she asked for his meaning, he told her his code name. "It means a person who makes something happen quickly, who speeds up something, especially an urgent something."

"Expeditor," she repeated. "For an important-sounding name, you do not give it an important-sounding definition. It does not sound somehow appropriate."

"You have another title in mind?"

"Yes. I was thinking, perhaps, of mass-executioner."

There was quiet between them for a time, Eagle concentrating upon the lap-lap-lapping sound of water against the bow and upon the movements upon the surface of the water. At first, he steered the little boat so that it approached the opposite shoreline, then he kept it moving relatively close by. His strip-watch said it was twelve-fifty. There were a good many miles and hours yet to go.

"I am sorry," she said finally. "What I said was not correct. You are merely doing your job. I—apologize."

He looked back at her and smiled. Both of them had stripped off the hoods and face masks to their suits. "There is no reason for you to apologize, Miss Yang. You are a scientist, one trained to help people build things, to progress. I am not a scientist. I am trained to destroy."

"Yet you are helping me."

"Yes. It was your father's wish—"

Her eyes brightened. "You met my father—when he was in America?"

He shook his head. "No. But his reputation is one of
118

excellence—and goodness—among the powerful people in my country."

"Your country," she mused. *This* is my country. This, the River Pei . . . the village near the place where . . ." Her eyes suddenly looked wet, but she forced a smile to her lips. "Will I like your country, Exped— Exped—"

"John."

"Your name is John?" she pronounced it as *Chon,* however.

"Yes."

"Is there more to your name?"

"Yes."

"But you will not tell me of that."

"That's right." He again smiled at her. "Do you know why?"

"I think I know, yes. It is in case I am caught and you are not. If I know your name—"

"You will not be caught, Miss Yang."

She laughed. "Why do you say that, Chon? Because such an event would mean you have failed your mission? Does not admitting the possibility preclude the event taking place? Or is it instead that you have some insight into the unseen workings of some spiritual world, and that you have divined what lies in the untold future?"

It was Eagle's turn to laugh. *"Preclude? Divined?* Tell me again how short a time it has been since you began the study of English."

"I am said to be a gifted student."

"I second the motion."

She looked at him without comprehension.

"Robert's Rules of Order. In the United States you can't get through a formal meeting without knowing them or without somebody seconding the motion at least ten times."

"A very complicated place, your United States."

"Not necessarily," Eagle replied. "Not if you handle things so that you can stay out of formal meetings."

"I am eager to learn your ways, Chon."

"You'll learn. You are, as you say, a gifted student."

She looked suddenly hurt, as if she felt he had been mocking her. Then very quietly, she spoke. "Chon, speak to me of matters concerning love."

He had turned to again peer from the front of the boat, but now his head snapped back. "Love?" he repeated. Simultaneously, Merlin's transmitted voice came at him: *You're to keep your hands off the girl.*

The girl: "Love, yes. I have been told that the— how do you say—yes, the *decadents* of the Western world think they know everything about love."

Merlin (in ghost form): Careful, Eagle!

Eagle: "You're the biologist, Miss Yang—not me."

The girl: "I was not speaking purely scientifically, Chon."

Merlin: I have warned you, Eagle, and you freely accepted the constraint!

Eagle: You'll have to elaborate further. I'm sorry, by *elaborate* I mean—"

The girl: "I know what you mean. Chon, I wish to learn the ways of your country quickly. That includes the ways between a man and a woman. You are a man and I am a woman. Thus . . ."

Eagle: "I'm not sure I understand you."

Merlin: You sure as hell do, boy, and I say knock it off!

The girl: "Well, after all, you call yourself Expeditor. You yourself have defined that as one who makes something happen quickly. All I am asking is that you live up to your important-sounding title. Is that wrong of me?"

Eagle (after considering the question): "I'm not certain that my employer—"

The girl: "You mean to tell me that the United States does not wish to teach other countries the truths of its philosophy of love?"

Merlin: I can see where your ideas are taking you, Eagle, and I insist—

Eagle: "My country, right or wrong."

The girl: "I do not understand."

Merlin: I do, Eagle, and I'll say this one last time—

Eagle: "Good."

The girl: "Good? That I do not understand?"

Eagle: "No. Good that even the spirits of the straightlaced must wither before a good old American proverb. I think we have a little time, you and I, to explore your education."

As she moved toward him, her fingers unzippering the front of her suit, Merlin's protests became fainter and fainter.

Orchid of Delight.

A name which was, at the least, appropriate.

Once, months—and eons—ago, John Eagle had been at the bottom of a sampan with a woman. They were on a river, not much different from this one, a river full of potential danger. The river was in Sumatra, the woman was Sumatran and named April.* She had not been inexperienced as was this girl, but she had given him release—wondrous release in a purely savage way. For that was what the Sumatran had been, a savage. This girl, however, was a scholar, but a scholar with a difference. Not your thick-glasses type in some university library worrying about large weighty theories—not in bed, at least. No, this girl . . .

Her figure was not as full as many he'd seen, yet as

---

* *The Laughing Death,* Expeditor #3

121

she stripped free of the plastic suit Eagle saw that any additional inches placed anywhere upon that supple frame would not have added, but detracted from her femininity. At first, her eyes remained lowered, the way she no doubt felt a proper Chinese woman behaves when disrobing, but when the act was complete and she was kneeling before him completely nude, she lifted her eyes to his face. Her smile was one of invitation and, now, as it was his turn to shed the artificial skin from the real, the smile became one of curiosity—then of appreciation, for already the love weapon of the man before her was rising to ready itself for the task ahead.

Gently, Eagle moved to her, arranged her body so that the plastic protective coverings of them both were beneath her. Then, very gently and slowly, he moved into a position preparatory to entry.

Merlin had been right about one thing. She was, as he had put it, a virgin *in tacto*.

"Now!" she gasped.

"In a moment," he replied. "You are not yet ready."

"But I am—I am!"

"Who is instructing who?" he asked.

"Whom," she corrected with a nervous laugh. "Who is instructing who-*ahhhhh!*"

He had still not entered her by more than but a fraction of his length. What she was feeling was the growth of that part of him which was placed at her entrance.

"Please, Chon. . . ."

"A moment, just a little more time." He was waiting to feel the proper degree of moistness, of heat, waiting also for her to begin the movement which would bring him slowly to her insides. The waiting was soon over. Slowly her hips began their movement, the unconscious movement which is instinctive to women even the first time they engage in lovemaking—instinctive if they relax and let nature take its course. Western women, at least most of them Eagle had known, did not have this talent for forgetting their own ego, for relaxing and simply being the women they were born to be. Indian women, Arab women, Latin women and other Asian women Eagle had known—they had none of the hang-ups of the European and American. It was perhaps a very good thing his job called for travel, Eagle decided.

Her breath was coming swiftly now, matching the rapid rhythms of her lower parts. "Chon, I—" But she stopped, his palm gently covering her mouth. He knew from her eyes that the cry of pleasure-pain was welling up within her, and although he knew that her cry would have added to her enjoyment, especially as she recalled the moment in later years, he also knew there was no undue need to attract attention to the sampan which lazily now drifted downriver.

Her body suddenly stiffened, then relaxed, then began a new slow churning movement. He released his hand. She smiled at him with her lips and through eyes which seemed to have become glassy. "The American way—it is good."

He smiled back at her. "You are easily converted."

"And you? Do you know much of the Chinese way?"

He looked at her with mock seriousness. "What might *you* know of that, little Orchid?"

Her slow movement continued, one which was beginning to affect the whole of him—a slow tantalizing, grasping, gripping, releasing, undulating motion which seemed matched to the gentle movement of the boat itself. Or perhaps it was her movement which was causing the movement of the vessel. Eagle was not about to bother analyzing that part of it.

"I am Chinese, after all," she said teasingly in answer to his question. "And I have read many books on the subject."

Eagle laughed in spite of himself. "Sex manuals? I would have thought they'd be outlawed—against the law—in the new China."

She nodded, still smiling. "They are, Chon. They are illegal. But part of our early training concerned how to win converts over to the communist line of thinking. As youths many of us were instructed in the tactics of what you call the underground press. Quite simply, we put our own underground press to work."

"Grinding out sex manuals?"

"*And* Confucius *and* Lao-tzu *and* other worthies!"

"No need to get excited," he told her.

She laughed. "But I *am* excited, a fact which you well know. But now I must see if all that reading did me any good—the reading and the practicing. Let us see if my Chon can become excited too!"

"Practicing?"

He asked the question warily, because suddenly she had stopped moving. She was motionless, while he—*he*—was ready to thrust mightily—

"No, Chon. Lie very still. Please. How else will I know if I have the proper talent?"

He obeyed her wish, his body reluctant to do so, but his mind still firmly in control. "Practicing?" he repeated.

She nodded happily. "The body, Chon, has many muscles. We of new China, as you call it, are very conscious of our muscular power. Even in old China, according to what I have read—ah, there!"

There.

Eagle felt something grip the extreme end of his tool. Not all of it, not its full length, just the very tip. Not hard, but not soft either. Somewhere in between. A steady grip. Then release. Then—

"There," she said. "Did you feel that?" But before

124

he had a chance to reply, she had done it again—that, and something else. A kind of brushing sensation, as if a very soft hair brush had been run along the shank of him. "And this, Chon? Do you feel this?" *This* was not a separate feeling but one in addition to the others. Almost at his very base, at the place where her lower lips surrounded him, those lips converged gently, tightly, somehow pushing him, pulling him, a fraction of a centimeter deeper within her. "Well?" she asked.

"I've never had a better argument for reading," he said, grinning.

And then the grin faded as the whole process began to take over his body. Grip, release, grip, stroke, tighten, loosen—all with no motion of her hips. As for his—"No, Chon, you are not cooperating!" she said tauntingly.

Merlin's ghost: You'd goddamned well better cooperate—Chon! After all, you got yourself into this.

"Well said," Eagle murmured.

"Chon?"

He stopped the movement he had begun, knowing full well that, in any case, it wouldn't have made much difference. Any second now—what with the tantalizing stroking movements she was using to attack his shaft—he knew that—

He exploded within her.

She lay back, relaxed.

And she laughed.

He laughed with her. "For a novice, very good."

With a mock affronted look, she asked, "Not excellent?"

Eagle shook his head. "One never tells a beginner that she—or he—is excellent. They immediately stop trying to improve."

She looked at him seriously. "The boat, Chon—it is still—"

"Fine. Right on course."

"And you—"

"Did the heroes of your sex books ever quit after the first time?"

"No, but books after all are merely books."

"The boat is fine," he said levelly.

It began again. He had begun to go limp, but her internal rubbings and soothings soon changed that. This time, when he emptied himself, she recognized the signs of it coming and leaned up to laugh into his ear at the precise moment of truth.

"Very good?" she asked afterward.

"Very good."

"Excellent?"

"Not quite yet. However, you haven't been very fair, you know."

"To you, Chon?"

"To yourself. You began by inquiring into the American way, and then suddenly you switched to the Chinese—"

"I see. You are right, of course. But you—"

"I, like the boat, am fine."

"You—"

But she didn't finish, because now suddenly there was something inside of her which had not been there before. Instead of the passive tool of this American there was something else—rather, *it* was something else. Bigger, stronger, a weapon of such proportion and length that—

"Chon!"

"A bit quieter, my Orchid—just a bit."

She opened her mouth wide to scream, but again his hand was there—softly but firmly. And not being able to seek release that way, she realized that her body had chosen another outlet. This wild thrusting within her—she would meet it with force of her own. She lifted herself up to meet the next thrust of him, and he went

126

into deeper depths than she even suspected she possessed. "Chon!" she whispered with urgency. "Please—Chon, no!"

But he didn't answer her, not with words. His actions answered, those plus the smile on his taut lips. "Chon—no! I cannot take any more, I cannot! Please—"

And then all went black for her, instantly she found herself in some dark lightless cave. She was lost in the darkness, wandering, searching for light—light—

Light!

It exploded about her like a thousand suns brought to being. Like the old New Year's celebrations with wondrous flame and color and sparkling life. The world renewed—a wonderful, painful, oh-so-pleasurable—

"Chonnnnnnnnnnnnnn!"

Later, as they lay side by side and as he stroked her body, she told him: "Such a feeling, Chon. It frightens me. I am afraid of you, I think."

"Of me? Afraid?" he asked in a whisper. "You did not enjoy it, then?"

"I—yes. I believe I enjoyed it. It was—"

"Very good?"

She smiled. "It was excellent, Chon. It was excellent."

He moved from her.

"Chon—"

"Get dressed! Quickly." And now she saw that he was pulling his own plastic suit onto his body. *"Very quickly!"*

She moved to obey. "There is something wrong?"

"Patrol boat. Looking us over, by its actions. It could be nothing, but—"

On the other hand, it could be something. That was what Eagle was about to tell the girl. But there was no need.

The need was made unnecessary by the bright beam

127

of light which suddenly was trained on the sampan's prow. It was followed quickly by a mechanical-sounding voice. A megaphone. Eagle looked to the girl for translation.

"He says for us to show ourselves. He says for us to be quick about it."

"All right. Show yourself. Tell him you're just a simple—"

"I know what to tell him," she replied. Moving to the front of the small boat, she pushed her head through the opening until it was bathed in the light. She began speaking. When she stopped, the megaphone began again. Eagle did not like the sound of it. For good reason, he found, when the girl whispered the translation.

"He says for the other person to show himself as well. He says he knows that I am not alone."

Knows? Eagle cursed to himself. Of course. It didn't take much of any kind of special engineering knowledge to see that the boat had not shifted in the water all that much when Orchid had moved to the front. But while she could show herself, he simply didn't look the part.

"Chon—they're getting closer!" she hissed, frightened.

Eagle could see that from the space between the tarp and the side of the boat. He made his decision swiftly. "Jump, Orchid—now!"

He rose fully upward within the tarp, falling forward as he did so. His ears caught the sound of a splash into the water, just before he felt the little boat toppling. With a sideways leap to the rear, his feet touched deck only for an instant. The crouched muscles of his legs straightened and his body cleaved the water like a knife.

The spattering of machine-gun bullets followed him like raindrops.

CHAPTER 13

"Chon!" the girl screamed, her head breaking the surface.

"Get your head down!" he roared at her. *"And use the hood—and the unit behind your knee!"*

A new volley of chattering hailstones splashed the water around him as he swam violently toward the girl, moving around so that the half-sunken sampan was between him and the gray patrol boat, splashing wildly so as to attract the attention of the gunner toward him and not—

The girl!

Where in the hell was she? He had not taken his eyes off her, but he couldn't see—

Of course! Slipping under water he adjusted his own hood and mask and put the plastic glasses over his eyes. When he came up, she was near him.

"You worked very fast," he told her.

"Fear sometimes adds speed to one's motions," she said in return. He could tell that the fear was still with her.

"Stay where you are. Every once in a while give the boat a little push." Those were his instructions as he went under—under the water and under the flooded sampan.

He remained underwater, reaching and sweeping back his arms in mighty heaves. The gun above him was quiet, but he had no doubt that the gunner was there, using whatever keenness of eyesight he possessed to spot a possible target. The men aboard the patrol boat were no fools. They could anticipate their quarry's diving underwater. What they could not anticipate, however, is that that same quarry could come to the surface and not be seen.

Silently, he did—just as the machine gun roared out another burst of fire. Just as silently as before, Eagle swam steadily toward the boat.

The machine gun was mounted on the foredeck and appeared to be able to sweep a full three hundred and sixty degrees. With the maneuverability of the boat itself, the single gun was enough to be very effective. Excellent, Eagle thought to himself as his fingers came into contact with the slow-moving hull.

Another burst of fire—answered by pellet-like thuddings into canvas and wet wood. Orchid was doing her part really well. Now it was his turn. His hands went upward.

As without a sound he stepped upon the metal deck of the boat, he grinned. There were but three Chinese on the boat—the gunner to the front, the man at the wheel, and the officer who held the megaphone. The officer had his back to Eagle, then Eagle had the back of his left hand—abruptly—to the officer's neck, his right hand being busy with something at the officer's belt. As the megaphone dropped with a *clang* to the decking, the wheelman whirled. Something stiff and hard and steel thrust forward and caught him in the throat directly under the jaw. He joined the officer in the sleep of death.

Meanwhile the gunner had turned fully around, the

130

barrel of his weapon ready for anything. But there was nothing, nothing for him to see at all except—*except*—

The officer's sidearm. His automatic pistol somehow was floating in midair! How could this be?

The question, of course, was never answered with any satisfaction, because as the gunner strained his eyes forward for a closer, surer look, the automatic fired. Just once, but that was quite enough.

Eagle dumped the three bodies over the side of the boat, then he picked up the megaphone.

"Miss Yang—just where in the hell are you?"

The patrol boat roared at full throttle, dead-on in the middle of the Pei, on a southwest course. Eagle looked at his strip-watch. One-forty. A long time until dawn, but a long way to go. Orchid, too, seemed concerned about the distance.

"The motor, Chon. You will destroy it if you keep it going at its utmost the way you are doing."

"Maybe," he admitted. "But I figure that, long before the motor dies, we'll have to abandon ship."

"Why do you say that? If you guided it more—more *clandestinely*—that is the word I wanted. In any event, if you did that, we might be able to get through with this boat."

"No, ma'am, that's not the case." He pointed to something to the left of the wheel. "You're fairly good with words—I mean, *clandestinely* and all. What would you call that?"

She laughed. "That's easy. That's a radio."

"Very easy," he admitted. "And on—at least it was when I boarded."

"On."

"Working—open channel to somewhere, probably another boat. If I know my officers, the late captain of this vessel was real quick to report that he'd zeroed in on us."

131

"Us? You think they know who we are?"

"Colonel Chou, maybe," he said. "At any rate, they —*they*—know there's somebody on this river to be watchful for tonight. We have one possible advantage if the *they* were north of us when our man put in his report. If not, we'll be having company real soon. Even if so, all it will take is a message to patrol boats south of us—which will be sent, believe me. Therefore, it's only a matter of time."

"And within that time you wish to make as much distance as possible."

He laughed. "You especially like walking?"

She laughed with him, then quieted. "The old Chinese, Chon, they say that one should not call up devils. Do you understand my meaning?"

He did. The Apaches had the same belief. Do not mention a specific kind of illness, because if you do, that illness—or its spirit—can hear you, and that gives it the entryway into your body. And in this particular instance it appeared the Apaches—and Orchid—were right.

Some fractions of a second before her eyes caught them in the moon-swathed night, he had seen them.

The patrol boats. Four of them, gray and gun-laden, coming straight from the south.

"How's your skill at gunnery?"

"I've never—"

"How about steering a boat?"

"The same, but I'd rather do that. If I can have my choice—"

"Take the wheel, Seaman Yang!" he yelled at her as he stepped onto the foredeck. "And take this too!"

She grabbed for the spinning wheel, then her hands reached up to catch the thing he had thrown at her. It was the patrol officer's pistol. "What am I to do with this?"

"Fire at will—in *their* direction," he laughed. "Either that or put it into one of your pockets."

"No!" she replied, pouting. "This garment fits me like a skin. To put something like that within it—it would be extremely unfashionable!" She lay the gun to the right of the wheel which she grasped with difficulty. "Chon—I do not know how to control this!"

"It works just like an automobile!" he called back.

"I have never *driven* an automobile!"

"Just point the bow—the front—toward where there isn't anything. And keep that throttle open."

Enough instructions. Either she had the idea or she didn't. If he'd thought about it, he would have had her try to steer the craft earlier, when he had the time to correct her mistakes. But he hadn't thought about it and she—

"Easy!" he shouted at her, regaining his equilibrium. "No jerking the wheel—not unless I say so. All right?"

"It will have to be," she said, accepting that fact.

Eagle nodded and adjusted the sights on the long-nosed machine gun.

First there were the roars of their motors, then the flashing lights. Two of the boats—those more centrally located—flashed them. Signals, no doubt. Signals to slow down or to halt or to open voice communication channels. Eagle considered sending back some kind of flashing response—anything, merely a response. That would serve to confuse them, maybe. And maybe it also would gain a couple of minutes before they swung into an attack. But however much time he gained, he would lose as much or more by slipping back to the wheel where the light signal controls were located. Then, when the ruse failed he'd have to climb back up to the gun again. As for the signal, Orchid perhaps could—

But no, he wanted both of her hands on that wheel. Speaking of which—

"Good!" he called back to her. "Hold it steady, then run for whatever opening they give us. *And put your mask on!*"

The boat weaved as she obeyed him, but he was ready for it. He was ready for the other boats' guns, too, when they opened up.

The signals blanked out first, then the two pairs of boats seemed to move to what was a semi-flanking position. Four spiders inviting the fly into their watery parlor. And the fly was accepting the invitation with all full speed as the hosts hovered ahead. It wouldn't be long now.

It wasn't. All four guns opened up, their initial marksmanship rather poor. It was the situation of the train all over again. Nobody had caused the military all that much trouble in recent years except for a little skirmish now and then. And men who train without expecting to use their training in life and death combat do not pay too much attention to those details of training which spell the very difference between life and death. Eagle's own training, however, had been far different and, although the weapon he now aimed at the nearest boat to the right was one he'd never fired, his marksmanship was a little better than that of his opponents.

His initial burst was a bit low and to the left. The second burst was directly on target. The on-deck gunner spun around twice before he crashed over the glass wind screen and onto the deck proper. A new hailstorm of bullets crossed Eagle's front as he now swung his weapon to the near left. His machine gun spoke and the gunner on that vessel stood straight up, throwing his hands into the air as if praying to some moon goddess. Then he went down and rolled from the deck into the black water of the Pei.

134

Within seconds now Eagle's boat would be in the center of the four, and seconds after that they would be chasing him instead of trying to cut him off as they were now. Eagle grinned as two sprays of bullets sailed past him. The two remaining gunners were frantically trying to knock him off before they were gunned down, but they were in no way the targets he was seeking. It was the two inner boats he was concerned about and—yes, the Chinese on board them were doing precisely what he'd expected them to do.

Three-men crews on boats like these can be very limiting in an all-out fight. Knock off the gunner, and all you've got left is the wheelman and the officer with no one to handle the gun unless either the officer or the wheelman takes it over. In the present circumstances, Eagle had expected the officer to command the wheelman to the fore, the officer himself taking the safer job of guiding the craft. He was fifty percent correct, for on the boat to his left that was precisely what was happening. The officer on the right, however, either did not have the air of authority to make his wheelman obey him or instead was himself a gutsy little bastard who insisted on doing his own killing of this foreign fool.

Either way, Eagle could not have cared less. He took careful aim, then squeezed off a burst to the right, then another to the left. The gunners on the two boats probably were startled, but not as much as the men who held the wheels, when the bullets crashed through the windscreen and found their targets—the two men controlling the vessels. Both veered violently, one of the boat-lurchings sending the gunner end-over-end and into the drink. The other gunner scrambled to the rear, almost making the glass before Eagle zeroed in on his back with a full burst of six.

Like kites which had broken free from their restraining strings the two unguided boats skimmed the water, one almost taking out the closest boat of the other two remaining. But the pilot of the outside vessel had a skillful hand, and the collision Eagle had hoped for never took place.

But now his weapon swung out again, almost directly to the right. Any second now and they were through! But first—

Two rapid bursts. One gunman down and out.

Now to the left—and to the left rear! *They'd done it!* Still, however, the machine gun spoke. And another gunner pitched into the river.

Eagle scrambled back to the wheel. He placed his hands over Orchid's. "I'll take it now. You can let go."

She closed her eyes. "That is not quite true, Chon. I cannot let go."

It was true. Her hands had gripped the wheel so firmly that her fingers seemed locked around it. Checking the location of the two manned patrol boats—they had swung into a position some forty or fifty yards directly behind him and were keeping up a steady pace—he gently freed her fingers.

"Did—did I do all right, Chon?"

"Miss Yang, we are both still alive and we are both still afloat. Does that answer your question?"

"You are a strange man, Chon," she said, and at that moment he wished he could see clearly behind the plastic glasses she wore.

But he couldn't. He smiled. "You're not all that bad yourself," he told her.

"As a fighting companion—or as a companion in a sampan?"

"Both," he said. "Decidedly, both." He smiled again. "And that, Miss Yang, is a very good thing, because the fighting is not yet over."

"I know that, Chon. And what of the lovemaking? Is that over?"

"Miss Yang," he said. "The people on board those two boats to our rear—no doubt at this very moment they are radioing ahead for other units to intercept us. We will see them most shortly, I am certain of it."

"As am I. But you did not answer my question. You admire my abilities in combat—in war. Do you admire my abilities in—in *peace?*"

"That's a title of a very famous book."

"I know. *War and Peace.* Tolstoy. A Russian, yes, but I have explained to you the workings of our underground press—"

"All right. Then you can see my point. The order Tolstoy put the two things in his title. He did not write *Peace and War.* First war, then peace. Understood?"

She hesitated. "You are, as I have said, a strange man. I shall await the peace, but I shall hold you to it—I promise you that. When the war is over—"

She stopped, knowing that he no longer was looking at her. Knowing full well that his eyes were far downriver.

Where, black specks now on the horizon, the line of patrol boats was swiftly moving at them, carrying the war the two of them had spoken of—war, and death.

"Chon—"

"Quiet." He cocked his ear. "We're in real trouble now, girl."

"The boats."

He shook his head even while seemingly denying the motion. "The boats, yes. But worse. Listen. What do you hear?"

"Hear? Why nothing, I do not hear—" And then she stopped, because she did hear it. The motor. The motor of their boat. It was running full steam, but an unsteadiness had crept into its churning.

"We're running out of gas," Eagle said levelly.

The timing was going to be crucial, Eagle knew that.

137

Already the gasping motor had begun to slow down their forward motion. The two boats behind them were beginning to shorten the distance which separated them. And to the front, the six vessels coming in a line upriver were beginning to tighten their formation.

"Make sure your zippers are zipped," Eagle told the girl. "And put that gun in a pocket—I don't care how you think it looks. Nobody can see you except me, anyway."

"It's you seeing me that I care about," she protested, but she did as he said, watching him as he extracted from his own suit two purple grenade-vials. "Do you think you can hit them from here?" she asked doubtfully. Her Chon was a unique man, but she didn't think he was *that* unique.

"I'm not even going to try," he replied. He again checked the distances of the other boats from their own, then he gave the white caps on the vials several twists. He jammed one of them in the narrow space between the bottom of the windscreen and the fore-deck. The other he let roll loosely in the rear of the boat. "All right, Miss Yang. I trust that you are ready to abandon ship?"

As she nodded, he guided her to the side of the boat which faced toward the western shore line of the river. "Keep close to me—and away from those other boats. *Now!*"

They dove, their arms and legs beginning to move in strong strokes even before they touched the water. Eagle looked to his right where the girl swam beside him and smiled to himself. He had wondered if she had the requisite skill in the water. From the look of her, she had. And that was clearly to the good. This was no time for him to be using his knowledge of water rescue.

They swam steadily toward the shore for a full two minutes, then Eagle called to her to halt. He wanted to be sure. Not that it made all that much difference, really, but he had always taken a certain professional pride in his work. That was part of it. The other part of it was that he simply wanted to watch.

On an angle to the south, the abandoned patrol boat was behaving in an erratic fashion, zigzagging along the surface of the water, heaving and choking as the last dregs in its tanks were bringing up the dirt and crud which is always deposited on the bottom of a tank of any age. The two boats which pursued the crippled boat were closing in, but seemed to be hanging back, approaching it with caution. They had every reason to do so, having just experienced the unexpected with regard to that boat. As for the six vessels which were to the abandoned boat's bow, they had no special reason for caution—hence they were gunning in with full power. If Eagle had timed things correctly . . .

Fifteen seconds passed and, treading water now, Eagle grinned. It was going to be almost perfect. The boat they had left was now completely circled by the other eight, each of which was closing the distance steadily as the group of nine moved erratically to the south. Megaphones were in use now, shouting commands back and forth as the circle tightened. Then one of the vessels moved in to almost touch the near side of the empty boat's hull. The Chinese who had the task of moving from his own boat to the other prepared to step off, balancing himself precariously on the outer edge of the rail. He was in the midst of transferring his right foot when the first of the vials blew.

Even before the echo of the first explosion returned from the hills, the second vial let loose its stored-up energy. Within the bright orange suns there were lesser explosions of gasoline tanks. When the suns died, there was little evidence of there having been nine boats on the spot. There was a place out there where the water seemed to be steaming hot, and there were bits of floating debris. That was all.

In the water next to him, the girl turned her face from Eagle. "How many men?" she wondered out loud in a voice that was as cold as the water probably was, although they could not feel it. "How many men just died on those boats?"

It was like the old joke: How many people in that cemetery are dead? The answer was: All of them.

Eagle did not think the answer all that fit in the current circumstance. Instead he touched the girl's shoulder and nodded his head toward the shoreline.

A large beam which was to be used in the building of a half-completed dock now served as their drifting mode of transportation, the girl holding onto its front and Eagle onto its rear. Before locking onto the floating transport, Eagle had given the girl one of his food-water pills, taking one himself. His body did not feel hungry, but he knew it needed sustenance, and here was a good time for it. There in fact was nothing else for his body to be doing. Well, that wasn't completely true. There was, of course, the lovely Orchid. But the beam was no sampan, and he would just have to wait.

Dawn found them drifting past the point where a tributary of the Hsiao flows into the Pei. When Orchid identified it as such, Eagle confirmed in his mind the calculations he'd already arrived at. At the same rate of speed, they would reach the juncture of the Pei and Sui River by nightfall. Still following the Pei, and still assuming a constant rate of speed, they would be passing the city of Chiang-men around dawn of the following day. From there they would be within four or five hours of the place they were to be picked up.

It all sounded very easy, but there were two things wrong.

140

One was that they could not expect to keep hugging this hunk of wood for all that time. He himself might have the physical stamina necessary, but the girl, he was sure, didn't have it. For all her strength, she had not been trained for such tests of endurance. Her body would require a number of hours of sleep between now and the time they reached the South China Sea.

The second thing wrong with the timetable was that it was too fast. According to Eagle's original calculations he was to have reached the target for destruction the fourth day he was within Chinese borders. He had in fact reached it the night of the third, destroyed it then, and had retraced a good amount of his steps southward by river. It now was only the fourth day, the morning of the fourth day. He'd been too damned efficient. The way his current timetable looked, they would reach pick-up point by tomorrow, sometime around noon on the fifth day from entry. Which would mean he would be a bit early for rendezvous.

Almost two full days early.

"Miss Yang," he called forward. "I think it's time for us to stretch our limbs."

CHAPTER 14

They moved on foot, half-running, half-walking, until Eagle's strip-watch showed the time to be ten in the morning. Then they rested for half an hour, taking to their feet once again. At noon, they found a thick copse of trees for a resting place. The girl collapsed against the trunk of the first one which seemed to her to be sturdy and strong enough. He took the mask from her face and pulled back the hood from her head.

"When you said it was time to stretch our limbs, Chon, I thought you had something other than walking in mind."

Removing his headgear, Eagle looked at her curiously. "Do you feel up to it?" he asked.

She smiled. "Swimming and running and walking perhaps have their own rewards, those which I am not in a state of mind to fully appreciate. But then I have been swimming and running and walking all my life. As to this other, I have just begun to try it. In my first attempts, I found the rewards most satisfying." She looked at him with eyes which seemed to smolder. "Or perhaps it is not the woman's place to ask? I am not fully aware of the customs of your country, as you know—"

He moved to her, his hands touching her shoulders. "As to that, Miss Yang, we do not happen to be in my country."

"And as to the other?"

But she needn't have asked. His fingers already were at work on the zipper under her chin.

Afterwards, he let her sleep for a full hour, finding an inward satisfaction in watching over the girl whose beautiful face in sleep still wore the faint smile of pleasure. When he woke her, he found that she was still able to keep up with him in their southward trek. At three, they returned to the river. For a time they swam, then hitched a ride on one of the ever-present barges going south. As they relaxed physically, Eagle's eyes continually scanned the river for patrol boats. There did not appear to be any more of them plying the water than there had been the previous day.

When night came, they again swam for a half hour, then as they had the previous night they spent a short interlude in a stolen sampan. It was all too short from the girl's point of view, but Eagle insisted they leave the sampan behind and move on foot again. "That's one thing they probably will be alert to—a drifting sampan," he told her firmly. Yet they were not bothered during the short time they inhabited the vessel and even Eagle wondered whether he was being overcautious. He dismissed the thought as soon as it entered his mind. There was no such thing as being overcautious, not in this kind of game.

Close to dawn they again took to the river in order to pass the place of rough waters where the Sui plowed its way into the Pei. Eagle was satisfied with the time they were making now, and he was more than satisfied with the way they were using up the hours they had to

143

spare. At noon, they left their unaware host who piloted a flatboat and took to shore and, in an unattended portion of a rice field, he and the girl made love again. "Am I getting better, Chon?" she asked as her internal muscles delicately excited the full extent of his sexual weapon. "Is it a compliment you seek?" he asked her in return. But as he emptied himself within her, she shook her head. "No, Chon. *That* is all the compliment I require."

The cycle continued. Run, walk, swim, make love. Through that day and the night, it went on, but Eagle reflected that neither of them was getting bored by the repetition. In fact, the intense physical activity which moved them consistently southward seemed to better prepare each of them for the romantic interludes which were spaced correctly in terms of psychological renewal which in turn made them more ready for the physical interim which would follow. It appeared now to Eagle that the purpose of the movement itself was nothing more than to bring them to the place where their bodies could again be joined. It was a good way to look at it, regardless of the practical realities which held the truth. Once during the afternoon she talked him into breaking their routine when they came upon an especially verdant patch of thick grass. He yielded to the temptation.

The grass patch was at the top of a sloping hillock which visually commanded in all directions a full landscape of rice fields. After they had disengaged themselves from each other, the girl looked over the land and the workers who toiled there. Her eyes were moist.

"This, Chon—right down there, all around us—this is China. Not the guns of the army, not the more wily weapons of those such as Colonel Chou, not even the universities where my father and I learned the skills of our calling. This—those fields and the people within

144

them—this is my country. It has been so for centuries, since the dawn of time, and it will be so long after the petty squabbles which separate nations have ended."

Eagle nodded but said nothing. He understood the sentiment, but he was not of such an optimistic view. It was this same stock of people who, centuries ago, crossed the land bridge which now was but islands between Russia and Alaska and who, through time, became the ancestors of the race of people who had raised him. The American Indian might have voiced a sentiment very similar to that he'd just heard. The season of buffalo comes each year, as does the season of planting and that of harvest. The white man and his vile depredations to the buffalo and to the land, they are but temporary things. They will go away, and things will revert to their natural patterns. But the white man hadn't gone away and now, as Eagle looked down upon the rice fields around him, he was not all that certain that the armies of the new China and the men such as Colonel Chou were such temporary things. If the rice fields and those who tilled them could not have been blotted out in all the previous centuries of Chinese history, perhaps the reason was because there had not been, until this century, weapons existing which could do the job. And he was not thinking solely of the bomb. No, there were other weapons which could be just as thorough.

For example, the Death Devils of Colonel Chou.

"It's time," he said grimly. "We've still got some distance to cover."

The hour was somewhat after midnight. The seventh day had begun. They had reached Chiang-men the previous day and from there they had cut across land, heading south-southwest, passing T'ai-shan late in the day. As they neared the coast, Eagle could smell brine on the winds from the water. It was a good feeling. To

145

the girl, he knew, it contained a sad feeling, but she did not speak of it. Only that once, on that patch of green grass, had she talked of her land and her people. Eagle was certain that, in her mind, they were behind her already.

He watched her now as they lay side by side within the shelter of an abandoned dwelling place which no doubt had belonged to a fisherman's family in days gone by. He watched as she looked out upon the water and at the fishing fleet of small junks which were anchored in varying distances from the shoreline. The smell of fish was everywhere, but the fishing village itself was quiet. There was no sound from the men whose bones and muscles no doubt were demanding and receiving the rest they needed after a hard day upon the water and before another to follow, no sound except the lapping of the water upon the shoreline—that and the breathing of the man and woman who were concealed in the ramshackle structure at the outskirts of the village.

At twelve-thirty, he told her it was time. Silently they moved to the water's edge, then into the sea itself. With steady strokes they swam beyond the first line of junks, straight toward the one which Eagle had chosen prior to their departing the shack. Although it appeared to be in no better shape than the others, it was positioned correctly—at least in Eagle's view. It was near the outside perimeter of the anchored vessels. If the need came for them to move out quickly, he did not want to be in the tangled center of all these vessels.

When they were on the deck of the empty boat, Eagle insisted the girl swallow one of his sustenance pills. Then they made love. And then they slept.

He awakened her gently as the first of the small dinghy-type boats left the shoreline. "Chon?" she asked. It still was dark. He placed a finger over her lips. "We're going fishing," he whispered to her.

"What hour is it?" she asked him.

"Zero hour," he said. He showed her the strip-watch. The sweep hand was no longer moving. It, like the other two, had been stopped at the twelve. The position of all three hands was deliberate, for Eagle's stopping the mechanism had started another—the silent signal beam which would guide their pick-up men to them. He had explained this to the girl before-hand, and she had not understood the actions he had proposed to take. "Why do we board the fishing boat? Why do we not simply await the boat which comes for us?" He had shaken his head. "A submarine, Miss Yang, is not a vessel one *simply* brings to the shoreline. We're going to have to meet our friends halfway—at least, part of the way."

They watched as the five men boarded the junk. Sturdily built men with hard-muscled arms and legs. As the first one stepped upon the deck, the girl touched Eagle's arm. He looked at her hand then into her eyes. He knew what she was thinking. He shook his head no. No, he saw no reason why he would have to kill any of these men.

The little fleet of six junks was on its way two hours before dawn. It traveled straight out to sea on a wind-ward tack, the wind coming from the southwest. Eagle nodded. It made little difference which way they moved. The sub would find them. Fifteen minutes later, however, Eagle spotted what might be a major complication. Two large patrol vessels were moving toward them from the rear. A routine movement, maybe, but if their big guns happened to be nearby when the sub surfaced—

No real problem for him. The sub could easily take out the two Chinese patrol boats. The problem was with these other boats. He had told the girl that there would be no more needless deaths. Not in actual words, but he had told her nonetheless. But it was not so much that he wanted to retain her faith, it was that he himself wanted no more innocent people to die. And if a shooting war opened up right here in the middle of these slow-moving junks—

Eagle's thoughts stopped dead as his eyes caught a slight change in coloration at his left wrist. The face of the strip-watch was turning a dull green in color.

Eagle's signal had been answered.

His head jerked back to the two patrol boats. There was no doubt now—they were heading directly toward the fleet of junks. He stood, his mind clearly made up as to his next moves. Motioning for the girl to stay exactly where she was, he moved swiftly to a position directly behind the man at the tiller. His voice sounded like some eerie wind:

"Hooooooooooaaaaaaaaaahhhh. . . ."

The man turned, his face confused.

"Hoooooooooaaaaaaahhhhhhh. . . ."

A trace of fright passed over the man's features. It was more than a trace as Eagle grasped the tiller and gave it a full yank.

The Chinese screamed, then shouted to his companions. When Eagle was sure they all were looking at their shipmate with curiosity, he brought up his left foot in a wide circle. It connected squarely and hard with the side of the tillerman's right shoulder. He appeared to be flying across the deck of the boat. Then Eagle sang out again, but this time in a loud voice:

"Hoooooo-aaaaaaaaaaaahhhhh!

Eagle had no idea what the Chinese word for *ghost* was, but he was sure it figured prominently in the shouts the startled men were now exchanging. Still, his demonstration plus their superstition had not yet combined to produce the action he wanted—and those patrol boats were getting closer by the second!

All right—he'd give them the grand show. He reached down to the small pocket behind his left knee.

The chameleon unit had one other characteristic which Eagle had found useful before. If the thin wires were reversed by the small switch on the bottom of the unit, it worked in reverse—far from blending the suit's wearer into the background, it made the suit blaze forth in the brightest color tone in the spectrum which was directly opposite to the background color. Eagle pushed the switch.

Then he threw his hands over his head and his lungs roared:

"Hiiiiiihhhhhyyyyyyyyeeeeeeeeaaaaaahhhhhhhh!"

Their answering screams began even before he'd finished. In a mad scramble, the five Chinese were over the railing and into the water, still screaming for their comrades on the other boats to pick them up.

Eagle grinned at the girl, as he turned off the reverse unit. Then he moved to the tiller. He'd gotten the crew separated from the boat. Now he had to separate the boat from the others. With a quick jerk of the rod which guided the rudder of the vessel, he began to move the junk into a long turn. From the others—and directly toward the oncoming patrol boats.

The three sails of the junk snapped into full balloons as the wind to Eagle's back caught them. Good. The wind was with him now, coming directly into the sails. If he kept the tiller positioned properly, he could move straight-line between the space provided by the oncoming patrol boats. But he knew better than that. They weren't about to let that happen. Whether or not they connected what was happening here with what had taken place upriver, Eagle had no way of telling. But these were not the boats—nor the men—which patrolled the river. These men would be better trained, and they would have quicker reactions. Nonetheless he had to smile when the first commands reached his ears from the electronic megaphone.

The girl was at his side. "They are saying—"

"I don't doubt it," Eagle said, cutting her off. "Just hang on, girl."

"Chon—you cannot outdistance them?"

He nodded. It was good in a way she could not see the grin on his face. "Just hang on. And keep down— the guns these boys are carrying are a little heavier than those we've faced so far!"

As if punctuating his statement the patrol boat to his left front fired a warning shot across the prow of the junk. Eagle looked quickly over his shoulder. The other junks were well away from the scene of the action now. With them safe, he could now concentrate on the business at hand.

Again the patrol boat on the left fired a warning shot, this one a little closer to the junk. "They will sink us!" the girl cried.

"You're probably right," Eagle said. "Unless we sink them first."

"But we have no weapons!"

"We've got one. You're standing on it."

The widening of her eyes told him she understood. And it was none too soon, because now the big gun of the second patrol boat fired. But this was no warning shot. It tore off half of the foredeck.

It was time for Eagle to make his choice. He chose the boat to the left. For one thing, it was closer. For another, its megaphone was still screaming commands. Eagle counted to five slowly, then he yanked the tiller, aiming the junk precisely where he wanted it.

Directly toward the patrol boat.

"Get ready to jump!" he told the girl. "Head for the second boat. I'll meet you there. Now—*jump!*"

She was too confused not to obey him. As he watched her body knife the water, Eagle turned back to the tiller, one hand gripping it tightly as the other extracted a green-colored vial from within his sleeve pocket. He placed the cap between his teeth and turned it sharply to where he wanted it, first to the right, then back to the left. A double-edged sword. The thing was set to go off on impact, but if there was no impact great enough to blow it, it would detonate in two and a half minutes. In Merlin's laboratory, one could have his cake and eat it too.

Both patrol boat guns were active now. The time for warnings was long past, and both were zeroing in for the kill. But as the wood crashed around the lone pilot of the junk, he laughed. They were good but not all that good. And they were too confident. Maybe, from their viewpoint, justifiably so. After all, what chance did a weaponless junk have against two war vessels? None. And Eagle's thoughts went back to something a Japanese friend of his once said:

"Curiosity, John, may have killed the cat, according to your Western proverb. But confidence—that can kill the tiger!"

Eagle's mouth suddenly tightened. The same could be said for the eagle. He had made, he realized, a serious mistake—in all his goddamned confidence, he had done something that could cost him his own life! The grenade-vial which rested on a battered wooden ledge to the left of his shoulder. It was set on *impact!* If one of those gunmen got real lucky—

There was no time for further thought. Only time to leave this goddamned junk by the quickest route possible!

He took the railing at a leaping dive, his cupped hands reaching for water seconds before he reached it. Then all of his muscles were working in fierce harmony. The thing now was distance—as much as he could—

The explosion seemed to lift his body clean out of the water. Shaking his head to clear it, he looked back as what remained of the junk nestled what remained of the patrol boat. Eagle laughed out loud. The stupid bastards. The stupid Chinese bastards—*they* had decided to ram the *junk!* They had done his work for him.

He jerked his head around. The other patrol boat now seemed to be stationary. Its engines idling, it appeared to be considering what its next move should be. Excellent—if the captain took enough consideration time to allow Eagle to—

Enough speculation! He moved, his arms and legs efficiently and strongly bringing him swiftly to his new target. While he moved, his eyes scanned the surface of the water for the girl. She was there, close to the patrol boat. Too close. If he had the time to do what he hoped to do, she was too damned close!

With one hand he motioned for her to move away. She fortunately had been looking for him, saw him and understood the frantic gesture. As she swam from the patrol boat, Eagle again took up his swift pace. She was nowhere to be seen as he touched the hull.

He moved around to the side of the craft, his hand removing from his suit one of the purple vials as he did so. Again his teeth came into play. *Click, click, click.* Etcetera, until thirty seconds' worth of time had been clocked into the explosive device. Good. Lifting himself upward, he hung onto the railing as with a deft hand he gingerly placed the grenade on a folded canvas tarp which lay directly beneath it. Then he pushed off.

His mental count had reached fifteen when he spotted the girl. She was twenty yards from him—but swimming back toward the patrol boat. "Orchid—*no!*" he shouted, but it was obvious she neither saw him nor heard him.

There was no choice. He had to intercept her.

He struck out, his arms and legs smashing the water furiously. Twenty seconds, twenty-five . . . six . . . seven . . .

She screamed as his hand clasped her thrashing ankle and brought her straight down—straight down into

152

the choking, coughing reality which came from unexpected submersion. But better that than to be up on the surface when—

The *when* took place, the din of it temporarily deafening both of them, the total absence of sound being followed by tinkling bell-like music. Eagle took her up.

"Chon!" she sputtered, her single word sounding over and over again in his brain: *Chon Chon, Chon Chon. . . .* She was dead tired, and he had to support her now. She wouldn't last long this way, he knew.

"It's all right," he told her, looking at the patrol ship which no longer was there. "It's all right. Now, all we have to do is to find a certain submarine. . . ."

He turned the chameleon units to nonoperational so that they could be seen. Then he looked at his stripwatch. It was bright emerald green. The sub was very near, he knew. If so, where the hell was it?

And then it broke the surface. It was a football field's length away from them. And then—the eternal megaphone:

"Mr. Compton? Are you there, sir? Mr. Compton?"
Eagle waved. The sub moved toward them.

Five minutes later, the captain of the vessel shoved two glasses of brandy at his guests. "Our employer," he told Eagle, in what was unmistakably a British accent, "had this placed on board especially for you. Here's cheers!" He lifted his glass, then noticed that Eagle's glass had not lifted.

"You were right there all the time," he said levelly.

"Oh, right, sir. All the time. Put on a rather good show, you did. My crew and I enjoyed it immensely."

"Enjoyed it, yes. Helped out, no."

The Englishman savored the brandy with his tongue, then he looked at Eagle curiously. "Good sir, my orders were to pick the two of you up. My instructions

153

said nothing about engaging the Chinese navy—even a part of it—in battle. Besides," he said cheerfully, "you seem to have done an excellent job of it."

"With little thanks to you—which is my point."

"I see," said the captain. "Well, I'm sure our employer will understand, sir."

Eagle looked at him. "Understand?"

"Yes, sir. If my conduct has been such that you cannot abide spending any more time upon my vessel, I am sure he will understand why you chose to take your departure now. I must say, however, that it's an awfully long walk—or swim—back."

Eagle stood up, but a hand restrained him. It was the girl.

"He is only making a joke, Chon!" She held up his brandy snifter to him.

"Not a very good joke, Miss Yang," Eagle said. "Not a very good joke at all."

CHAPTER 15

It was a fascinating place, this place the submarine had brought her to—she and the American who had taken her from her native land. She did not have any idea where it was, nor did she know how long they had spent on board the submarine. The place was some kind of cave, or at least one of its entrances had allowed the underwater vessel to enter it directly. Once they had debarked from the sub, they had entered a white elevator. She had thought they were moving upward, but she couldn't be sure. The American she knew as John—she suspected the name Compton was not his own, she didn't know why—or any of the others who received them, they said nothing regarding their whereabouts. She understood why, of course. It was not merely that she was Chinese. This was the kind of place which no one knew about, unless they had specific business within its confines. She suspected that the numbers of people with that qualification were very few.

Yet it was the kind of place she immediately understood. Everything she saw seemed white and clean. Sterile, like a scientific laboratory. Yes, much of the place was devoted to research. Of what specific kind, there was no real clue, but now that she had seen the wonders of the chameleon unit and the plastic suit it controlled, now that she had experienced the sustaining powers of the little pills and had seen the deadly effects of the curious little vials of colored solution, she ventured that she could form a fairly accurate guess as to the nature of the research.

They were ushered into a room with several screens to the front of it. The American called it a "briefing room" and told her to sit, that shortly they would be hearing the voice of his employer. Shortly, they did. It was a strange voice, a mixture of ancientness and great power.

"Good morning, John."

So—another fact: wherever she was, it was morning.

"Sir," John said simply.

"And good morning to you, Miss Yang. I trust your voyage was pleasant."

"I was made very comfortable, thank you," she replied. She looked at John and smiled. Somehow his return smile looked somewhat—embarrassed.

"I see," the voice of the hidden man said slowly. Was there a touch of anger there? Possibly, but it was gone when the voice continued:

"Miss Yang, I have been asked by the President of the United States to welcome you to American soil. A number of people are working in Washington right now to prepare the necessary papers which will identify you as a citizen of our country. Also being considered are the details of a number of job possibilities from which you will be asked to choose. These will be as closely aligned to your own field of specialization as practical. You will be given enough time to make a decision based upon facts, and therefore your next two or three weeks will be spent traveling throughout the country so that you can make an intelligent choice which you will be happy with. There are certain restrictions, I might add, which are based upon considerations of your personal security, but by and large I am certain we will be able to accommodate most of your needs. In the meantime, my staff has prepared a number of films and videotapes which will assist in orienting you to the customs and habits of your new society. Whenever you feel ready to begin—"

"Excuse me for interrupting, sir—"

"It's all right, Miss Yang. You have a question?"

"I have several questions, sir. The insect project, have you located it? Did you find the place called *Chirkee?*"

There was a pause, then a slight hum. Then a section of the front wall of the room became a map.

"There is no harm in your knowing, Miss Yang. When John radioed his report from the submarine, we

156

fed the words *Chirkee* and *Chickee* into our computer along with climatic data regarding the area about Shih-hsing. You are looking at a map of Panama where, you will note, the word *Chiriqui* appears in prominence no less than five times. There are nine provinces of Panama, one of which is called Chiriqui. The southern shoreline hovers above a body of water known as the Gulf of Chiriqui. In the province located just to the north, that of Bocas del Toro, there is a city called Chiriqui Grande to the immediate north of which you will note a body of water called Laguna de Chiriqui. Finally, there is an extinct volcano in the far western part of the country which, too, is called Chiriqui."

"The volcano," the girl said. "That would not be an appropriate place."

The hidden voice seemed to chuckle. "You are correct, Miss Yang. Extinct volcanos may be appropriate for *some* things—I think John would agree—but not for the purpose of mass-breeding insects. Not at least in a natural-habitat situation."

She noticed a smile on John's face and wondered at the cause of it. Was her mention of a volcano all that funny? She again looked at the map. "Do you have data on temperatures and rainfall?"

A second map replaced the first. It was color coded so that it was simple for her to come to a decision. "It would seem to me that the northern part of the country would be most suitable for the purposes of the project. Although I have not actually seen firsthand one of the special strain of insects, it would have to have been compatible with the breeding conditions prepared for the others. Therefore, I would dismiss the southern portion of the country—the entire Chiriqui province and where it borders on the water marked Gulf of Chiriqui."

"Excellent, Miss Yang. Our computers agree with you. Which brings us to the northern section, namely the Chiriqui lagoon and/or the city of Chiriqui Grande."

A topographical close-up of that area was flashed onto the screen. Also something else.

She gasped.

"You said you hadn't seen it, Miss Yang. This is our Death Devil."

"Devil of Death," she said quietly. "Yes, the name would seem very appropriate." She looked at the new map on the wall. "But that is a very large area. Those highly wet areas—"

"Swamplands," the voice said.

"Yes, that is the word. There are many of them. I could not begin to distinguish between their characteristics. Was your computer able to differentiate between—"

"No."

There was a pause. Then the man beside her spoke:

"But you know where they are—correct, sir?"

"Yes, John, we know. If your report from the sub had been less thorough—if, to pinpoint, you had not mentioned the fact you had not seen the corpse of Colonel Chou Ko-chu at the scene of destruction—we might not be in the position to know. Fortunately, that gave us one thread. Fortunately too, the man is alive and well at this moment. Our agents were able to trace his movements from China to Panama. He is here."

A red circle appeared on the map indicating the eastern lip of the land fronting on the Chiriqui lagoon.

John nodded. "When do I leave?"

"You have two hours. You'll go by submarine to Camp Six, and from there to target by air. You will, I assume, wish to check out your weaponry."

"Yes, sir."

"*Sir—*"

"Yes, Miss Yang?"

"It is my intention to accompany Chon."

Eagle looked at her with surprise. "Miss Yang, I don't think—"

She cut him off, her oval eyes flashing at his, then turning to the place on the wall from where Merlin's voice had emanated.

"It is not that I have any doubts regarding Chon's ability to do the task required. I, above all, should know of his abilities. But it is simply that he doesn't know what to look for."

Merlin's voice was level. "We have agricultural specialists who will brief—"

"On the techniques *we* have used? I doubt that seriously, sir. I would venture to state that I am the only chance you have of locating the breeding grounds."

Eagle nodded. "You, of course, could tell me what I need to know."

She smiled. "I could, yes."

"But you won't."

"That is correct. Because, Chon, it would not be complete. I could not, in two hours, give you a full course in entomology. No, I must accompany you." She again looked up at the wall speaker. "You, sir, must realize that I am as much a specialist in my work as Chon is in his. In addition, I have my personal reasons."

"Colonel Chou," Merlin said.

She repeated the name as if it was venom on her lips, then quietly added, "Also I have a debt to repay your country. I wish to begin my life in America by earning my keep. Chon will tell you that I can handle myself, that I need nothing in the way of special consideration on his part. This is something I must do, even if that were not the case."

159

Merlin seemed to be thinking it over. When he spoke it seemed to Eagle to be a last-ditch protest: "I gather you have parachuted from an airplane, Miss Yang."

"Chinese women learn many skills. Yes, sir, I am completely familiar with that act, having performed it many times."

Merlin sighed. "The people in Washington will not be happy about my letting you risk your neck, I want you to understand that."

She smiled, aware now that victory was hers. "I ask a thousand pardons for placing you in difficulty with your superiors, sir, but it is my neck I am risking. We of China, as you may know, do not hold individual life to be of so great an importance."

"We of America do," Eagle said.

"In that case, Chon, when we return I shall try with all my heart to learn your American ways. They—in addition to those I have learned from you already—are intriguing." Again she looked up at the speaker. "In the meantime, sir, I would appreciate speaking to one of your people who understands insect life."

CHAPTER 16

Thirty seconds after they had splashed into the black waters of the lagoon, he was by her side. He also was hopping mad. She on her part was smiling cheerfully, even while she spewed out water and was trying to disentangle herself from the 'chute.

"Do not be angry with me, Chon. I made it all right."

"Angry? Goddamn it, woman, why did you lie? Why did you say you'd jumped before?"

"If I had not said that, you would not have let me come. Besides, now I can truthfully say that I have jumped from an airplane—can I not?"

"I should drown you," he said through his teeth. But instead of drowning her, he was in fact releasing her from her tangles, just as not that many minutes ago he had half broken his back jerking his sky-dive pattern to intercept hers so that he could straighten out her sails. If he'd not been able to, she would have cigarette-rolled her way downstairs to what would have been a splattering finish. Nonetheless, as he looked at her now, he could not help but admire this girl. Real guts. Guts which he wanted to remain distributed precisely

161

the way they were now. "Are you sure you're all right?"

"With thanks to you, yes. I always know that you will take good care of me, Chon."

"When this is over, lady, I may just spank the pants off you." He turned from her and began stroking toward the shore. The swim was one which had been calculated to take at least an hour and a half.

She moved up to his side. "Spank? That is not a word I know." When he told her what it meant, she laughed. "So—*that* is what you will do when I have my pants off! I think not, Chon. I really think not."

"Be quiet," he ordered her, but his tone was not as rough as he'd intended it to be. "Save your breath for swimming. You'll need it."

He struck out swiftly, moving through the water with a smoothly fierce crawl. If she intended to keep up with him, she was going to have to work hard—and, as he'd told her, breathe hard.

The night was totally dark and as they sliced through the water their plastic suits blended perfectly with the surface of the lagoon. He enjoyed the feeling of water on his bare head and the unmuffled sound of his movement. Within the next two hours, if things went well, he would once again be working in his role of destroyer. But now, right now, he was no more than a master athlete, competing not against other men but with the elements of nature itself. No, not really competing. The best athletes never competed with natural forces; they used them, they fused with them, became them.

It was at these moments—the brief times like these which formed a normal part of his assignments—that he felt his own worth. Expeditor. The title was more than that of a simple hired executioner. Other men could kill and destroy as effectively as he could— maybe. But it was the ability to get to the target area which distinguished John Eagle. And now he wondered how many jobs Merlin had turned down because they did not require the skills of his Expeditor. Little jobs, which the old man might shake his head over and quietly say no. He wondered, then smiled. No, Merlin wouldn't have declined on that basis alone; he no doubt would have had a very valid excuse that his Expeditor was, at the moment, quite busy. For, in the time since the contract with Merlin had received John Eagle's signature, there had not been too many idle moments. Not that Eagle had any cause to complain. If he, like Merlin, had an employee commanding Eagle's salary, he'd get his money's worth—he'd work the living hell out of him, keep him moving.

Moving. Eagle grinned. Be an Expeditor and see the world.

For just as long as you can stay alive.

His shoulder muscles flexed as he reached out for the handfuls of water in front of him more rapidly now, with more strength. For three full minutes he kept up this almost superhuman speed, then he relaxed to enjoy the blood pounding through his system and the air pumping through his lungs. The thought of air—or breath—reminded him that he was not alone. He stopped and turned.

At first he couldn't see her, she appeared so far behind him. He was about to go back to meet her, but then thought better of it.

He was lazily lying on his back when she swam up to him. She could hardly get the words out:

"Am . . . I . . . detaining you?"

"Oh, no," he said cheerfully. "It's just like you told my boss. You need nothing in the way of special consideration from me. I just wanted to be sure you didn't sink to the bottom wearing that suit you've got on. My employer, I'm sure, would figure a way to dock its cost from my salary."

"Your salary! Up—*up the dragon's rectum with your salary!*"

"Colorfully put. You must instruct me one of these days in the niceties of Chinese swearing. As for now, Miss Yang, we press on."

With which, he rolled over to his stomach and began moving again. However, he kept his pace in line with hers. John Eagle, Mr. Nice Guy. Up the dragon's rectum, indeed!

Silently they moved from the water into the marshy cluster of green plant life. The girl found a place of substance to seat herself and rested as Eagle detached from the small of his back an elongated parcel constructed of the same material as that of their plastic suits. His face was one of complete satisfaction as he opened the parcel and took from it a pistol.

It was the familiar CO_2 pistol which had been his weapon on so many assignments. It was good to have the whispering weapon within his grip again. But it did not stay in his hand for very long. Checking to be sure it held a complete clip of its steel death-needles, he attached it to the left side of his utility belt. His concentration now was upon the two lengths of metal he extracted from the backpack. With an economy of movement he screwed the two sections together. This, of all his weapons, was his favorite. With the strong alloy bow he was deadly accurate, but it was more than just his mastery over the weapon which gave him the sense of power he always felt when notching an arrow in the steel bowstring or, when as now, he was engaged in stringing the bow itself—a particular feat he'd never seen another man do—no, the special feeling which came to him when he touched this weapon was that of the power of the red man, the power of the Apache warrior.

He checked the plastic quiver which contained twen-

164

ty steel-tipped arrows and attached the top of the quiver to the receiver tab which was part of his suit, a tab just below the back of his right shoulder. When the bow was looped over the left shoulder so that a simple jerk downward with his left hand would "draw" the weapon into his fist and be ready for action, he nodded to the girl.

"Let's find the enemy," he said softly.

She looked around her. "You are certain this is the correct place we have landed."

"Near enough. We were dropped precisely and my compass should have brought us fairly close to where the men to whom Colonel Chou came to see are headquartered. It would stand to reason that the insect beds are nearby."

"But I do not see this house—or shack, I believe your employer called it."

Eagle looked upward toward the hill. "It's here, somewhere. I saw some lights as we were swimming in. But never mind that. That's my concern. Yours is to locate the reason we're here."

She smiled at him. "You can help do that too. Here, take this." From her jacket she pulled out a small metal box. When the box had opened, she handed him two devices. Two similar devices she kept for herself. "Your people are very clever," she said. "I had but to explain what I wanted, and it was provided most swiftly."

She pointed to the smaller of the two things, something which resembled an earplug, which was precisely what it was. "Place that into your ear," she told him. When they had both positioned the plugs, she touched a small lever on the second unit which was some kind of sound transmitter. The sound Eagle heard from his earplug sounded like a high-pitched sort of scratching.

"That is the sound which the Devil of Death makes. Fortunately your people studied the available specimens quite thoroughly. All you need to do is to play that sound, again and again. It is when you hear an answering call, that is when you have located the nests—or those adults which are there."

"Very clever," Eagle said. "However, it seems that you could have told me all this before—before we left."

"Yes, but then you would have come here alone, is that not right?" She gave him no chance to reply, but pointed her two hands in opposite directions. "And now that I am here, there is no reason for us not to hasten our task. It occurs to me that it would be best if we conduct our hunting separately."

He had the objection on his tongue, then thought better of it. She was right. There was no telling how long it might take the two of them, moving together, to locate the breeding area. By splitting up they would cut the time in half. "All right. We'll do it your way. But get that hood and mask in place—and turn on your chameleon unit. And, Orchid—"

"Yes, Chon?"

"We are here to wipe out insects. That's the first task. If you meet any devils on two legs, keep away from them. Do you understand me?"

"Yes, Chon."

He gave her final instructions—that if she found the nest, she was to look for him; that if an hour passed without her finding the nest, she was to again retrace her steps back to this point. Then they parted. As they did, if Eagle had been able to see the gleam in the girl's eyes, he would have changed the arrangement—drastically.

The big man was known as Snake. Not *culebra* or *sierpe* or *serpiente*—not any of the Spanish substitutions—but the English. Snake. Such was how he preferred to be known, this big man with hands that could

166

crush lesser men to death with a thick finger and a thumb, and what he wanted, he normally got. The name he had chosen for himself had little to do with his physique, but with his frame of mind. "The snake, she is deadly. The Snake, he too is deadly."

His associates were the first to agree. There was that matter of his size, his strength. But there was also something about the man's mind. Crazy, his comrades were certain. Dangerous-type crazy. The man's pets, for instance.

Snakes. The interior of the one room building over-looking the lagoon was filled with the cages. The walls were lined with them. Inside were several varieties of the reptiles—several sizes, several colors—but they all had one thing in common. All were killers, just like the man who called himself by their collective name.

Except at the moment, in the dim light of the lone kerosene lamp, the man called Snake did not look at all threatening. Even so, as he paced the room, trying to explain himself to his important guest, the other men—the nine who were there—moved anxiously from his path while trying hard not to come too close to those deadly cages. "They are caged!" he would roar at them when they responded nervously to his pets. "And they are my allies, which makes them your allies also. *Is that not true?*" *Sí*, they would answer. *Sí, es muy verdad!* But they never seemed to make it sound convincing enough, which they suspected was precisely to the big man's liking. At any rate, he found their responses worthy of the deep-belly roars of a laughing bull.

But now he appeared almost meek as he tried to put his case to the foreign one, the one with the yellow skin:

"It is with sad heart that I tell you this, *Señor* Colonel, but this sadness which I feel—really feel deep down in the insides of my stomach—this sadness I cannot allow to come between the truth and your ears. The truth, the sad truth, is that once again I must be asking you for additional funds."

The colonel, seated in one of three rickety chairs which graced three sides of a rusted metal kitchen table, nodded with an understanding look. Actually, Colonel Chou was most uncomfortable. He did not like these Latin self-styled revolutionaries, not at all. Their dedication was limited only to what they could get out of this business for themselves. Their methods—and their manners—were as unrefined as the lowest of animals. Next to one of them, the commonest Chinese peasant was an individual of delicate tastes.

The man called Snake threw up his hands. "You see how it pains me to say these things to you, Colonel? It pains my men as well—is that not so?"

All of the others nodded their heads. "*Sí*—it is so."

"But," Snake said, his head shaking sorrowfully, "the truth must be made known. Otherwise I would not be doing my duty, is that not so, Colonel?"

Colonel Chou paused before answering. "I believe a recent payment was made—one which was intended to take care of your needs for many months to come."

"True, Colonel. True! But, alas, the money has been spent for many things incidental to our important work. The work of conversion, as you may know—conversion of those who are undecided in their political beliefs—that is not always inexpensive. And the work is not becoming more easy. Those of the Cuban, those of Castro who would follow the Russian bear, they come to us telling us that they are the true communists and not ourselves who are loyal to the much-revered city of Peking. They come waving money, Colonel—money! And it is my sad lot to say that some of those people whom I had almost convinced that ours was the way—they slipped through my grasp as if I had but the strength of a weak fly-paper! The thoughts of Mao are

168

precious, good Colonel, but they are not fully appreciated by men who have their eyes upon the Russian ruble!"

Snake sighed. "Yet we do what we can. Sometimes, in the really difficult cases—especially when one who has been loyal to our cause has gone over to the other side—I have them brought here. For education, you see. See there—upon that wall. Some of them have remained there while I have tried to educate them."

There were two rings in the wall. Hanging from them were thick rawhide ropes, stained with blotches of dark red. On a shelf a distance away were a number of implements. Colonel Chou noted the thick whips and a number of curiously shaped knives. Again the thought came to him that he did not like this place or the people who lived here.

Again Snake sighed. "But, alas, I am no educator, Colonel—not in the face of my obvious poverty and the poverty of even my most loyal followers. Those I have brought here for training for the most part have died with their hands held by those ropes." He smiled toothily. "Or sometimes, my little pets were let loose upon them." The smile faded. "All of which is a very, very sad thing, do you not agree?"

Colonel Chou nodded. "You shall have another payment."

Snake grinned, clapping his hands. "You see?" he said to his men. "You see and you hear that? Didn't I tell you that the good Colonel from Peking, he will not let us down?" When the automatic nods followed, Snake turned to the colonel. "The payment, she will be a big one? The work is so very large, you see, and—"

"It will be totally adequate," Colonel Chou interrupted.

"Ad-e-quate!" Snake repeated. "Ad-e-quate! Ah, the word is like music to my humble ears. *Ad-e-quate!*"

His eyes narrowed slightly. "I am certain that one meaning of the word is *muy grande*—in the translation?"

"You may rely on that," the Colonel said wearily. These filth! Holding him up like this—he was no better than a common highway thief or a bandit warlord of the olden days! Colonel Chou's insides were churning. He seriously doubted that Snake and his people had even met a Castroite. It was nothing more than a ruse, nothing more than an excuse to practice their own method of extortion. But all he'd have to do was to put up with their disloyalty for just a little while. When the insects had been bred and were on their way, he'd have no more need for Snake and his men.

Colonel Chou would very much enjoy the task of killing them, the big man first. A bullet straight to the gut, then another in each eye. Then . . .

But that was a pleasure for the future, even though the anticipation of that pleasure was helpful in getting him through these difficult present months. Now, however, he had to be certain that the primary work here was going well.

"The incubation beds—when were they last checked?"

Snake furrowed his eyebrows in thought. "Yesterday, I think. Or was it instead the day before yesterday? Piño—when was it the incubation beds last were checked?"

A tall lanky man seemed to give the matter thought. "Yesterday, I think. Or perhaps the day before. It is like you said."

Snake's grin was wide. "You see, Colonel. Yesterday —or the day before. The beds, they were checked then."

Colonel Chou's voice was brittle. "In that case, I wish them checked tonight. Now."

"Now?" Snake asked. "Now—in the dark, *Señor* Colonel?"

"Your man Piño is afraid of the dark?" Colonel Chou asked.

The room was hushed. All were waiting for some sign as to how the Panamanian leader would take the question of the foreigner. He laughed. They laughed. He laughed again.

"Afraid of the *dark?* Colonel, the heart of Piño there—that man's heart is blacker than any night possibly could be. You may take my word on it, Colonel, he—"

"I shall take your word on it," Colonel Chou replied. He looked at his watch. "Now, if you will kindly have those beds checked, I think I should like to get some sleep. I know that each of you has a woman somewhere you would like to return to. Thus I suggest that you go about your proper business, and I shall see you in the morning."

Snake looked at him curiously. "You wish us to leave you here—alone?"

Colonel Chou smiled. "We Chinese are peculiar people in that regard. We cherish a certain amount of privacy." He looked at Snake with an amused expression on his face. "Is it that the powerful Snake has no woman who would welcome him into her bed this night?"

Two of the men began to laugh, but something in Snake's eyes stopped them dead. The big man himself then laughed—but it was forced. "A woman. A—*one*—woman? I beg the *Señor* Colonel's pardon, but I have many, many—"

"Excellent. Then you certainly do not need to be entertained by my humble self any longer. Please, however, be sure that the insect beds are seen to."

Snake's face reddened. "You think we do not do our jobs?"

"If I thought that," the colonel said, "I think you would have known my thoughts before this."

Their eyes locked, then broke. Colonel Chou was satisfied that it was the Latin who had broken contact first. It had nothing to do with the man's fear or respect. It had to do with the money that the Chinese had said would be coming. One does not kill what the Americans call a "meal ticket" and that is what the Chinese colonel was. One does not kill nor does one dare to defy. There are limits, and this one called Snake had just now realized that he'd come dangerously close to exceeding them.

The big man laughed again. "My pets, Colonel—I hope they do not disturb your rest."

"Your hope is my hope," the colonel replied. "I know how attached you are to them."

The one called Snake again locked eyes with the Chinese. At first there was an element of doubt that the yellow man would dare even to touch his reptiles, but the doubt faded.

"You are," Snake said slowly, "an interesting man, *Señor* Colonel."

Colonel Chou bowed his head slightly. "I have survived much. I expect to survive much more. If the need should be, I would include snakes and *other* members of the animal kingdom."

In the back of his brain he recognized that he shouldn't have added that last part. In China, the deprecation would have been recognized immediately for what it was. But here, out here in this uncivilized swamp . . .

Snake merely shrugged. "I hope that time proves you correct, *Señor*. It is my very real hope that you are dead right."

The big man stalked to the door, his men following, leaving Colonel Chou to wonder.

The emphasis of the big man's words. What did he

172

mean? Within the borders of his own country where nuance was an art, Snake would have meant very clearly that he wanted the Chinese roasted alive. But here?

The thin yellow man shook his head clear of such thoughts. Very counter-productive at the moment. Right now he had to collect his own thinking, to be sure that—

A sound.

The door. The fools were not even civilized enough to close the door. But—

They *had* closed it, he was almost sure—

But obviously it now was open. Perhaps the catch was not properly—

Yet, he had not seen it open. But, after all, the light was not all that good here. The simple lamp—

What was that?

Some kind of *click! Within* the room.

Then he saw it.

A pistol—a revolver, one like those carried by Snake's men. Except that this one seemed to be floating in midair. Between him and the door—

"Prepare to breathe your last, Colonel Chou," a female voice said.

Chon would again be angry with her, she had known that from the time she had made her decision—which was made before they had parted. But Chon had his mission, an important one, yes. She on her part had her own mission. The insects could be located without too much trouble, but if the destruction of them was such as to provide a warning to the man who was her mission, he might once again have an opportunity to escape. And that must not happen!

So she had cut a path upward as soon as the American who called himself Expeditor was out of sight. She

173

would show him that she too could bring things to a hasty conclusion, that she too could—*expedite!*

She too had seen lights when they had swum to the shoreline. While the man had been checking his weaponry, she had calculated the direction. And she had been right. The house . . .

There was but one window in the face of the shack, set to the right of the door. There were several men inside, all of them speaking English. Her eyes pierced the dimly lighted room and there, seated at a table, she spotted him.

Colonel Chou.

Blood began pulsating through her veins, a smile began growing upon her lips. He was there, simply sitting there, waiting. While she—

She halted her train of thought, suddenly realizing that she had no weapon. With a pistol, right now, all she would have to do is take careful aim and fire through the glass. She could not have missed. But—

She had no gun. Nothing! How would she—

Again her thoughts were interrupted. The big man of the group—a man bigger and heavier than Chon, even—began to walk toward the door. The others appeared to be following—yes, *were* following. She shrank back against the side of the house, then she remembered.

The magic-like suit of plastic. As long as she was quiet, they would not know she was there.

The door opened, the giant-man passing out first. He halted, and as he did so her heart stopped beating, but it was only to grunt something to the others who jumped after him as if they were dogs Finally the last of them turned to close the door behind him. Her eyes watched him carefully for any evidence that he sensed her presence, but then those same eyes spotted a new point of focus.

The pistol the man carried.

174

It was in a weathered-looking holster, very loosely placed. If she could . . .

Her fingers reached out deftly, her thumb and forefinger grasping the chipped wooden handle of the weapon. Without a sound she lifted her hand upward and toward her.

The gun came with it.

The man turned the other way and stepped off.

She waited for ten full seconds before she allowed her lungs to explode the air which they had contained. Then she turned back to the window.

Her destiny awaited her still, seated at the table with a smug expression on his face.

Quietly, she moved to the door. Quietly, she opened it.

How very pleasant it was to see the colonel's eyes bulge at the sight of the pistol pointed at his breast. How very pleasant it was to deliver this creature's death sentence:

"Prepare to breathe your last, Colonel Chou!"

"Who—how—"

"Your vengeance has reached you, Colonel—all the way from Shih-hsing."

The man was trembling. "Vengeance?"

"For my father, the venerable Dr. Yang. For what you did to his name—and for what you did to his life!"

He shook his head as if to clear it. "I must be dreaming. That is it, of course. I have fallen asleep and am dreaming this nonsense. How else could I see a weapon appear in midair and hear the voice of one who could not possibly be here."

"I *am* here, Colonel Chou."

"Speak on, dream. You shall not disturb me, not now that I know what you are."

"Shall I shoot you—to prove you are not dreaming?"

He shrugged. "If you wish. I am, after all, in your control. But then, dying in one's dreams happens often to active men, I have done so before, and wakened immediately." He laughed. "A gun trained on me with no one holding it? Even you—speaker in my dream—must acknowledge the insanity of that!"

The girl's nostrils flared. The filth was right! What vengeance was there in simply pulling the trigger and allowing this man a death that he did not believe was real? With a frantic move, she did it:

She pulled off her mask and the hood from her head.

"Now, Colonel—now, what do you think? Am I still a dream?"

Colonel Chou rose like a bullet. "It's *you!* It *is* you!"

She smiled. "I am my father's daughter, and it is in his name I now pull this trigger. This world bids you a swift goodbye, Colonel Chou!"

"Not yet, *Señorita*," came the voice from behind her. Simultaneously a beefy hand struck out at her arm. The gun dropped to the floor as she turned and—

She caught it full in the face—the backhand slap of the giant Panamanian. As his grip on her wrist tightened, he laughed. *"Dios!* I have seen nothing like it! An invisible girl! If Piño had not discovered that his weapon was missing, and had I not brought some of my men back with me . . . well, *Señor* Colonel, I hate to say what might have happened in our absence!"

Colonel Chou nodded, his eyes fixed upon the girl. "It has to be something she's wearing. Get her out of it, whatever it is."

"Gladly, *Señor*," the big man laughed. "And then we shall ask her to tell us about this thing. I am thinking that maybe the ropes on the wall would help us, do you think so, *Señor?"*

"It will do as a start," Colonel Chou replied.

Long before he actually saw them, Eagle's sensitive ears had picked up their motion. Four of them. The little speaker in his ear had not spoken, but these sounds were louder and more meaningful than insect talk. These were men, men in a hurry, men moving toward an objective. And since Merlin's contacts knew of no other men close by the place Chou had been received, there were the best of odds that their objective was the very one he sought. He halted, freezing his movement. Waiting. And then, as he saw them come, he let them pass.

Like a ghost he followed.

Within three minutes, the speaker in his ear confirmed the fact that the four men were crouching near the place which was his objective. He smiled his thanks to circumstances. Then he drew his CO_2 pistol.

The gun whispered four times, then Eagle rose and went to where the bodies of the four dead men lay. "The fortunes of war, my friends," the Expeditor said. He removed the device from his ear, placing it into a pocket in his suit. Then, from the utility belt around his waist, he took three plastic bottles of a yellowish-colored liquid. The caps snapped off with the upward flip of his thumbnail. In seconds the entire area of the bed was covered with the liquid.

Eagle reached into his pocket again, this time for an object which Merlin's lab technicians did not have to invent—a match. But he thought better of it. No, first there were other details to clean up.

He looked at the breeding beds. If he had been walking by here at night with no specific objective in mind, he might have noticed the flat metal trays with

177

the wired criss-crossings at the top, but then again he might not have. The camouflage of the natural greenery might have completely hidden them from his conscious mind. But what did it take to breed insects, really? Even death-dealers like these—what did it take, once the research and cross-pollination had been accomplished? Nothing—nothing but the proper environment. He looked at the beds, not seeing with his eye, but with his mind's eye, the enlarged photograph he had seen twice now in Merlin's briefing rooms. Nothing very deadly to the naked eye, but in reality . . .

"You're killers," he said softly to the forms he could not see in the metal trays. "But your deadliness is not your fault. Tonight your spirits will ride the waves of the wind, and for this I ask your forgiveness. But let your spirits rest with the assurance that he who has caused you to be born will also die this night."

Necessary? Was it really necessary for him to speak his assurances to these creatures who could not hear his words? He asked himself that as he turned his back on them. He could not answer. But somehow he felt it to be the proper thing. His grandfather, the sage Ho-kwa-sikna, had expressed it once. "The animal should know he dies so that the stronger form of life can live. And through him, the animal lives. It is the way we hunt buffalo. It is the way we hunt men as well—except that the men do not have to be told."

Men. No—man. One man. That was the next target, and he would know why he was hunted, know why he was being killed. But first—

The girl. He'd have to find her and be sure she remained in a place of safety.

"You live now," he said, turning back to the breeding beds. "But later this night you die. It is for the best that you do."

Ten minutes later, Eagle found the signs. The signs that told him that the girl had not been searching for insects but for something higher on the hill. Cursing to himself, telling himself that he should have known better, he moved after her.

He hoped that he wouldn't be too late.

For her sake, he hoped, and for his own. And for any son of a bitch who had put a rough hand on her.

CHAPTER 17

Colonel Chou smiled at the nude girl who, in spite of the intense pain from the tight rawhide which trussed her wrists to the rings on the wall, still managed to hold fierce defiance in her eyes.

"Perhaps you will now tell us, delicate little Orchid, how it happens that you have come here this night."

Snake laughed. "She will tell us, *Señor*," he said. "You need not say *perhaps* about that. But, if you please, I wish to do the questioning myself. Out here, there are too few pleasures for men like myself."

The Colonel's smile faded. "Then I wish you would proceed. I am certain that she is not alone, that there is someone else with her—perhaps the same man who took her from my country."

Snake nodded. "In time, my good Colonel, all in time. But first I must figure out this strange garment. It appears to stretch, and I am thinking that I would like to wear it—so that I too might become almost invisible." He held it up between himself and the light so that the silhouette of the suit was clearly outlined. "Yes, but first I think I must become naked too." He looked at the girl. "That is the secret, is it not?"

The girl said nothing, did not move her eyes or her head, but the big man proceeded to rip off his clothing as if it were composed of tissue. When he was naked, his eyes darted around the room as if to dare anyone within to snicker at his condition. No one did. He laughed.

"Now—let us see. Yes, here . . . and here." His legs went into the proper places. After a little more experimentation, he had both arms covered. It took a little difficulty to find the front zipper, and even more to locate the hood and mask, but soon he was completely covered.

The Colonel was impressed. "It is a fantastic thing." He turned to the girl. "You will tell me how it works."

"Surely," Snake said. "She will tell us that, too, Colonel. Do not be so much in a rush. She will tell."

The slim man named Piño shook his head. "Snake, I do not wish to say this, but the suit is not too good if you stand where you are and I stand where I am. The light of the lamp, it does not go through—"

"I know that, *stupido!*" Snake said through his teeth. But quickly he moved against the wall. His eyes nodded. "Now, you so very bright Piño, you tell me what you see!"

"*Nada*—nothing, Snake. Except for the eyes, those I see really clear."

Colonel Chou rubbed his jaw reflectively. "Yet, when the girl first entered, I did not see her eyes. . . ."

Snake laughed. "In which case, *Señor* Colonel, there must be—ah! I have found it. How about now?"

"It is as if you have disappeared!" one of the Latins said.

"More than that," Snake added. "This little bit of plastic—the last part I put over my eyes—it allows me to see myself. My own hand and foot. You cannot see me, but I can see all of me. This suit is worth millions of *balboas*—and dollars, too—for, wearing this suit, where can I not go, in what great bank of money can I not take what I please to take?"

"Please—" Colonel Chou began. "The girl—"

The invisible Snake laughed with the roar of a bull. "My comrade from Peking, do not worry about the girl. I shall handle her. But it now occurs to me that I and my men no longer are dependent upon you for our bread and wine. This project of yours—these bugs—it is something I have never understood too good, and also it is a creepy thing. Always having to be sure the bugs are okay. No, I do not like it. And, to tell the complete truth, I do not like you, *Señor*. In fact, I have never liked you. Therefore, I feel that I now can do without you altogether. Luis—you do the honor. *Por favor,* please shoot the *Señor* Colonel."

"*Shoot?*" Colonel Chou asked, jumping to his feet.

But the answer came in the form of a shot. As the Chinese crashed into the wall next to the girl and slumped to the floor, a fat Latin—presumably Luis—replaced his smoking revolver in his belt.

"*Bueno,*" Snake said. "That will keep down the noise level just a little bit as I now ask the little yellow girl a couple of questions. Hey, little girl! Are you afraid of Snake? Don't be, don't be. These questions that I will ask you, I promise they will be very easy to answer."

The girl looked at him—or to the right of the door on the far wall where she assumed he was—with eyes of hatred. "I will tell you nothing!"

The men in the room chuckled, as did Snake. "You

see, little one? You see how my men laugh to hear you say what you say? That is because they know you are incorrect, very, very wrong. What Snake wants you to tell, you will tell. I beg a thousand pardons, little one, that we here are not as delicate in our torture as the people of your race, but with our humble knives and our whips we try our best—and we shall try now. But first, to save us both from a painful experience, I will ask you again. Will you answer my questions?"

"You have not asked any," she said fiercely.

"I just have asked you one!"

"Then I shall answer that one question. No."

The sound of a sigh came from the place where she assumed Snake to be. "You have said it, *Señorita*. You have said the one word which I do not enjoy hearing. *No.* A terrible word, one which causes much pain— pain which you will now begin to feel. It surely is a pity that—"

But he stopped. The sound of smashing glass made him stop.

Then the sound of screams which came from the throats of two of his men.

They were death screams.

Eagle had waited long enough. He had drawn up to the window at the precise moment a shot had been fired from within. He saw the Chinese fall to the floor behind the table set near the opposite wall.

He could not, of course, miss Orchid and, as her figure crashed into his brain, he had to cool down the rage he felt within him. There were five men he could see within the room, but the speaker was hidden from him, probably standing near the window or the door. To get a better look, Eagle took off the special glasses. After all, Orchid no longer was wearing a functioning chameleon unit. Five.

Five that he could see. Plus the downed Colonel and

182

the girl—and the unseen speaker who, from his tone, was obviously the leader of the pack.

All right. It was time to reduce the odds.

In one smooth motion, the bow slid down his left hand while the right pulled from his quiver an arrow which notched into the steel bowstring at the precisely right moment that the string presented itself. A quick but strong pull backward—and the arrow flew.

Glass broke and two men screamed—the two of them being close enough together so that the steel tip went completely through the gullet of the nearest and, since the second man was somewhat shorter, through his brain.

Hands moved to guns, but already a second arrow was in the air. There was no scream this time as the space between one of the gunmen's eyes was suddenly the repository of the length of shaft from Eagle's bow.

Three down, two to go, and the guns of the two were blazing. But the unseen target was no longer there— nor did the target anymore clutch the bow. Filling his hand now was the gas pistol, drawn from its place in Eagle's utility belt and ready—very ready—as its owner moved swiftly from the smashed window to the door next to it.

The sole of Eagle's foot exploded against the thin wood. As it shattered, the CO_2 pistol spoke twice its whispering death.

Two more dead. That left the unseen one.

The thought couldn't have been more to the point, although Eagle might have guessed it from the wild look in the girl's eyes. She screamed at him as he dove through the doorway, his gas pistol spraying its deadly needles all along the wall which contained the door.

"The suit!" Orchid shrieked. *"He is wearing my suit!"*

But her words were not necessary. Eagle understood

the situation immediately when something collided against his wrist and sent the CO_2 pistol skittering across the floor. And when the second thing happened, he knew that he was involved in what very well might be the fight of his life. The last fight of his life.

The second thing was heralded by the sound of something ripping.

The something was to the left of his head.

The place where his plastic eyepiece was—had been—connected to his hood.

"Welcome, *Señor*," a deep voice said. "Welcome—*to your death!*"

Eagle stepped backward, crouched low. An invisible opponent, an opponent who could see his every move, an opponent about which he knew nothing—size, weight, strength, movement. How—

Something blurred in front of him and crashed into his face. He stepped backward under the impact, his hands rising to protect his body for the follow-up he was sure was coming. It came—and caught him heavily on the left side of the head. Whoever his opponent was, he was strong—and he was big.

And he was not playing around.

The sudden blur before Eagle was low. It had to be a fast-rising foot. Eagle pivoted quickly to the right, then struck out with his own left foot. It touched nothing but air, but so had the other man's foot. Swiftly the Expeditor's mind blended with his bodily motions. His survival depended more than it ever had upon his reaction time—especially since his senses had very little to react to. Almost nothing.

No, that wasn't quite true. It was true that he couldn't *see* his opponent all that clearly, but there are other senses—hearing and smell, for example. And a man trained as an Apache hunter had those senses honed to a keen edge.

A shift in balance, a foot lifting from the floor—these actions cause sounds, and even as Eagle's mind registered them his body was in motion to avoid their consequences. Again what was a powerful foot-thrust missed its target.

And the sense of smell was active as well. The man smelled as if he hadn't taken a bath in months. No, the suit would keep most of that inside. It was the bastard's foul breath that assaulted Eagle's nostrils.

"Come on, tough man," he said. "You mentioned death."

"That is true, *amigo*, I mentioned—"

But the sentence broke off, the man instantly realizing his mistake in allowing his voice to give away his presence. He was only partially successful in avoiding the flying two-footed kick which Eagle immediately launched. The resultant crash beside the door told Eagle the present whereabouts of the man he could not see. He dove toward it.

Like a sledgehammer something cracked into Eagle's shoulders and he dropped to the floor—but like a leopard he was rolling and on his feet at the instant that two other feet thumped into the space he had occupied. Again he dove, but this time the other must have been ready for him, because he touched nothing on his way to the wall.

A snake cage rattled under his hands. The sounds of hissing were added to the others Eagle's ears sifted for information as he turned himself with a snap-pivot and a sudden step to the side.

Air rushed by the right side of his head, and his hands immediately went to the place. But if he had doubted the swiftness of the other, he was certain of it now. No contact—not at least in that direction. The fist smash to his face was contact a-plenty.

As it connected, Eagle's back crashed against another of the snake cages. More important, as that action was completed, Eagle's mind decided his next course of action. His hands dropped to his right side and gripped a heavy cage. It came up as if it was nothing—up and straight out.

It hit some obstruction. Eagle laughed. "Play with this one too, *amigo!*"

A second cage flew from Eagle's fingers, again connecting. But there was no third. The next thing which flew—or seemed to—was Eagle himself. Not directly at where he thought his opponent might be—but toward the doorway. Rolling and standing upright, he laughed again.

Now he didn't have to guess. The light from the lamp on the table was dim, but it was enough. The big man—yes, a very big man—was outlined beautifully.

What's more, the big man realized it.

"Don't move, *Señor*," he said grimly. "Make one move toward me and I open the snake cage. And then I place it very very close to the nicely formed belly of the girl."

Eagle assessed the man's chances of making it. They looked very good. But there was no reason to allow him to believe it too much:

"You're a dead man, friend."

"*Señor*, we all are dead men. It is our fate to die from the moment we are born. I do not meet death or its coming with fear. How about yourself?"

"Me?" Eagle laughed. "I've got nothing to fear at all. It's me who's doing the killing. As of right *now!*"

He launched himself. As he expected, the big man's arms flexed—and the cage flew. Directly at Eagle. It crashed to the floor by the doorway an instant before Eagle crashed into the man who had pitched it.

"*Señor—no!*"

But it was too late—Eagle's hands and arms had found their target and had wrapped themselves around the big man in a combination full-nelson-bear-hug. The man's feet were lifted inches from the floor.

"No, *Señor!*"

"I'm going to break your back, *amigo*. At least, that's my intention. But I might not do it."

Eagle's arms and shoulders surged with power as he tightened his grip and let the man feel a little of the pain it caused. "I might not," he repeated through his teeth. "Would you like to hear my conditions for not breaking your spine?"

"*Sí*—yes, *Señor*—yes!"

"The insect beds. You tend them?"

"My men—yes—*sí!*"

"How many are there? One or more than one?" This was a question he had to have answered. If the girl had done the job she'd been charged with doing, there would have been no need to ask. But then if she had done her proper job, there wouldn't have been a need for him to even meet this man—alive. "How many?"

"One—just one! It is a big thing, *Señor*—but there is just one place. *Señor*—you promised!"

Eagle had tightened his grip, but now relaxed it just a bit. "Yes. I promised—and I intend to keep that promise. Let's have a look at you—all right?"

The question was not much of a question since, before anyone could have answered it, Eagle had released the man with one hand and ripped back the hood of the plastic suit. The man yelled with pain as the mask was pulled down, then yelled again as Eagle's arms re-established their tight grip.

"What do they call you, tough man?"

"They call me Snake."

Eagle grinned. "Appropriate, very appropriate. You've got yourself quite a collection here."

"Please, *Señor*, I do not wish to speak of snakes at a time like—"

"But *I* do. And you want to please me, right?" The vise-like grip tightened still more.

"Yes! Yes . . . if you wish."

"Those in that cage there. Those little green things. Poisonous, I take it."

Eagle had jerked Snake's face around so that he could see the cage against the wall that he was talking about. "I *asked*—are they poisonous?"

"Why—why do you ask, *Señor?*" Snake asked cautiously.

Eagle's reply was matter-of-fact. "Because, my friend, I'm going to stick your head inside that cage. Your unprotected head. It wouldn't help me much if—"

"No—they are *not*—"

"That's a lie, *amigo*. I know the species well. You shouldn't have lied to me—that makes me angry."

He stepped toward the cage, the big man's body helplessly moving before him.

"No! You *promised*—"

"That I wouldn't break your back. I intend to keep that promise."

"No—no. Please—*por favor! Madre de Dios, no!*"

But the top of the cage was now open and Snake's bulging eyes were staring at the deadly coils of writhing green.

"Snake, you are a liar on another count."

"*S-señor?*"

"You told me about death. You do not meet its coming with fear. That's what you said. But your whole body is trembling."

"*S-señor!*"

"*Adios,* Snake."

As the big man's face was thrust into the top of the

cage, he screamed. He screamed again as his little friends attacked. It was a long, long scream. It died as he fell back to the floor unconscious.

Eagle turned off the chameleon unit. He looked at the girl.

She, on her part, avoided his eyes. "I know. You have every right to hate me."

"No," he said. He took a knife from the shelf beside the girl and sliced through the rawhide. "But concerning spanking . . ."

She rubbed her wrists, still not lifting her eyes to his. "At your leisure, Chon. I will submit to this brand of punishment if you deem it necessary."

"What I deem necessary is your getting back into your suit. Now."

"But—"

"It is being worn now by another. He is dead."

"And *naked!*"

"And he probably stinks like holy hell, too. But you'll do as I say."

She nodded. "Yes, Chon. Although I think . . . yes, I think I would prefer the other."

"Other?"

"Yes. The spanking."

But she did as he said. While she stripped off the plastic suit from Snake's body, Eagle retrieved his CO_2 pistol and examined the dead. All of them were satisfactorily so—except for one. Orchid's eyes snapped open wide as Eagle moved around to the wall side of the metal table.

"Colonel Chou," he said. "It's fitting that you should be the last."

The Chinese had been lying face down on the floor. Now he slowly pushed himself up to a kneeling position. The right side of his head was matted with blood. He smiled tentatively. "They are not good marksmen, these men," he said. "You will do better."

189

"I'll try, Colonel." Eagle raised his pistol.

"No, Chon—please do not kill him."

Eagle paused. The girl, now fully clothed in the plastic suit, stepped to his side and smiled down at the wounded man. "Please, Chon. I have promised myself this singular pleasure. I promise you that I will not make any foolish errors."

Eagle nodded, extending his gas pistol to the girl, handle first. She shook her head no, her eyes resting on the shelf of torture implements and the snake cages below them. "I'll not need your weapon, Chon."

Colonel Chou's smile was gone now, his eyes going from the woman to the man. "Shoot me now!" he urged Eagle. "Quickly and honorably, let this miserable life end!"

Orchid's voice was as cold as ice. "It will end, Colonel. But it will not be the quick and honorable death that you feel you deserve."

Eagle turned to leave. "Don't take too long. A helicopter will be coming for us as soon as they see the signal."

Outside, Eagle picked up his bow and began to move down toward the breeding bed, the frantic pleading of Colonel Chou still in his ears. As he walked, he removed a head from one of his arrows and replaced it with a special one from his utility belt. This arrowhead would burst into flame upon contact with its target. The target was the breeding bed which in turn would burst into flame. The fire would mark the end of this assignment and also would be the signal the helicopter pilot was looking for.

He stood now on the hill. Below him were the bodies of the four men. He notched the specially prepared arrow and pulled back the bowstring. He paused, the lines of his face grim.

The night was silent—except for the screams of

190

terror which were coming from the shack behind him.

He released the arrow and watched as man-made Death Devils died in the roaring fires of a man-made hell.

are you missing out on some great Pyramid books?

You can have any title in print at Pyramid delivered right to your door! To receive your Pyramid Paperback Catalog, fill in the label below (use a ball point pen please) and mail to Pyramid . . .

PYRAMID PUBLICATIONS
Mail Order Department
9 Garden Street
Moonachie, New Jersey 07074

NAME_____

ADDRESS_____

CITY_____STATE_____

P-5   ZIP_____